Better off without the Angels?

"You know, in some ways, getting these German measles might be the best thing that could have happened," Kimberly said. "I mean, now none of us will have to see a single Angel for at least twenty-four hours."

"Good point," I said. "And we'll definitely have a lot more fun at our slumber party than the Angels will at theirs."

"Hey, let's go into my closet and try on all my stuff and make up new outfits," Lila suggested.

"Too bad Mandy isn't here," I said. "I mean, making up funky outfits is her specialty."

"I'm sure we're perfectly capable of coming up with cool outfits ourselves," Kimberly said haughtily.

I raised an eyebrow. "Well, yeah, but—"

"I mean, Mandy's not the only one who has any fashion sense, you know," Kimberly went on.

Lila, Ellen, and I exchanged looks.

Kimberly's face was red with anger. "You'd almost think you miss the Angels or something, the way you can't stop talking about them," she spat out.

Bantam Books in THE UNICORN CLUB series.
Ask your bookseller for the books you have missed.

THE UNICORN CLUB™

TOO CLOSE FOR COMFORT

Written by
Alice Nicole Johansson

Created by
FRANCINE PASCAL

BANTAM BOOKS
NEW YORK • TORONTO • LONDON • SYDNEY • AUCKLAND

RL 4, 008-012

TOO CLOSE FOR COMFORT
A Bantam Book / September 1995

Sweet Valley High® and The Unicorn Club™
are trademarks of Francine Pascal

Conceived by Francine Pascal

Produced by Daniel Weiss Associates, Inc.
33 West 17th Street
New York, NY 10011

Cover art by James Mathewuse

ISBN: 0-553-48351-X
Published simultaneously in the United States and Canada

Bantam Books are published by Bantam Books, a division of Bantam
Doubleday Dell Publishing Group, Inc. Its trademark, consisting of the
words "Bantam Books" and the portrayal of a rooster, is Registered in U.S.
Patent and Trademark Office and in other countries. Marca Registrada.
Bantam Books, 1540 Broadway, New York, New York 10036.

PRINTED IN THE UNITED STATES OF AMERICA

OPM   0 9 8 7 6 5 4 3 2 1

112732

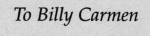

To Billy Carmen

One

"Hey, Mandy, why don't you join us today?" I asked in my friendliest voice as I came up behind her in the lunch line.

Mandy Miller looked back at me, squinting. "With you and Elizabeth or you and the Unicorns?" she asked suspiciously.

"With me and the Unicorns, of course," I answered as I picked up a tray and put it on the metal shelf along the lunch counter.

"Will you-know-who be there?" she asked, picking up her own tray and placing it next to mine.

I flashed one of my famous innocent expressions. "Who are you talking about?" I asked, wide-eyed. I knew very well she was talking about Kimberly Haver.

Mandy folded her arms and tapped her foot.

"Oh, OK, I guess she will be sitting with us," I

said. "But she really wants to try to make up with you." That wasn't exactly the truth, but I was desperate—the Unicorner just wasn't the same without Mandy. Besides, when Kimberly saw how cool Mandy looked that day in her plaid jumper and ankle-high lace-up boots, she'd probably beg her to join us. Well, maybe.

Mandy scrunched up her face as if she were trying to solve a hard math problem. "I don't know—"

"Well, I do know," I jumped in. "Just give her a chance."

"I'll think about it," Mandy said. "Maybe by the time they bring out the next pan of lasagna, I'll make up my mind."

"Great! Everyone will be psyched." For the first time in a while I was feeling optimistic about the state of the Unicorns.

Maybe I should give you a little background so you'll know what I'm talking about. First of all, my name is Jessica Wakefield. I'm in the seventh grade at Sweet Valley Middle School and I'm a Unicorn. The Unicorns are the prettiest and most popular girls in the school. At least, last year— when most of us were in sixth grade—we thought our popularity was our main claim to fame. We cared mostly about boys and parties and gossip and boys.

A lot changed this year. For one thing, Janet Howell left middle school. Last year she was in eighth grade and the president of the Unicorns. Once she left, Mandy Miller became the president, and the whole mood of the group changed. For instance, we started volunteering at this day-care center for poor children. I know what you're thinking: the *Unicorns* were running around after messy little brats? But like I said, we changed. We even opened the club up to my identical twin sister, Elizabeth, and her friend Maria Slater, who I used to think was pretty nerdy. We also let this new girl named Evie Kim join our group.

I couldn't believe it when Elizabeth actually agreed to be a Unicorn. She used to give me so much grief about the club. She was always telling me how silly and superficial she thought we were. See, Elizabeth's a lot more serious than I am. It's not like she doesn't have fun or anything, though. When she's in the right mood, she can be more fun than almost anyone else I know (besides me, of course). It's just that she's pretty serious about her schoolwork and working on the school newspaper, the *7 & 8 Gazette.* She wants to be a writer when she grows up, and she spends a lot of her free time reading mysteries.

As for me, studying isn't exactly my idea of a good time. In fact, I do as little studying as I can get away with. I love to shop, go to parties, and gossip.

The funny thing about Elizabeth and me is that even though we're pretty different personality-wise, we look exactly alike. We both have long blond hair and blue-green eyes. We even have a dimple on our left cheeks in the same exact spot. The only way you can really tell us apart is that I usually wear my hair down and Elizabeth usually wears hers back in a ponytail or in two barrettes. Oh, and I'm the twin with the better wardrobe. Elizabeth just doesn't have my fashion sense. I guess it's something you're born with.

Anyway, until all this Unicorn war stuff started, Elizabeth and I were absolutely best friends. Sure, we had our fights like all normal sisters do, but we were almost always on the same side.

But all that changed when Kimberly Haver came back into town. Kimberly, along with Janet Howell and a few others, was a member of the old Unicorns. She moved away for a while, then came back after school started this year.

Well, when she saw what had happened to the Unicorns, she nearly freaked. She couldn't believe we were visiting kids in a day-care center and taking people like Maria and Evie as members. She just couldn't believe how goody-goody we'd become. I have to admit, she had a point. I remembered how much fun the Unicorn Club was in the old days, when all we thought about was boys and parties and stuff.

Anyway, the problems really started when Mary Wallace, another Unicorn, ran for president of the student council. The Unicorns were all set to support her, but then Kimberly moved back to Sweet Valley and decided that *she* would run for president of the student council, too.

You can see why this presented a major dilemma for us Unicorns. How were we supposed to choose between Mary and Kimberly?

It was a hard decision, but each one of us made it. Lila Fowler, Ellen Riteman, and I supported Kimberly. After all, Kimberly stood for what the Unicorns were traditionally about, and tradition's tradition, right?

Elizabeth, Maria, and Evie thought Kimberly would be a bad choice for president, and that she was mean besides. They were on Mary's side. Mandy was the only one who wouldn't choose a candidate. Or at least she didn't choose one until the very end.

Here's what happened: Kimberly stole a copy of Mary's campaign speech, which outlined all of her ideas—and I have to say, Mary had some pretty great ideas. Kimberly read the speech in front of the whole school, pretending that she'd written it, and she won the election. Awesome, huh? Well, not exactly. See, Mandy told the principal, Mr. Clark, what had happened, and another vote was taken. That's when Mary won.

We were all so mad at each other about the election that the Unicorns split into two groups. Elizabeth, Maria, Evie, Mary, and Mandy became the Angels, and Lila, Ellen, Kimberly, and I still call ourselves the Unicorns.

There are a couple of things I really hate about how the club's broken up. One is what's happened to Elizabeth and me. We're acting practically like strangers. The other is losing Mandy to the Angels. She's one of my best friends, and the Unicorn Club just isn't the same without her.

If she'd just hang out with us a little, I bet she'd see how much she misses us. I mean, we're much more fun than the Angels. OK, so it wasn't all that nice of Kimberly to steal Mary's speech, but no one's perfect, right?

"What's so funny?" I asked as I plopped my tray down at the Unicorner. That's what we call the table we sit at every day in the lunchroom. Obviously I'd missed a big joke. Lila was laughing so hard, she was coughing on her milk. Kimberly's face was as red as the tomato sauce on her lasagna. Ellen was holding her stomach as if it were about to burst. I felt like I was watching a foreign movie without any subtitles.

I sat down next to Lila. "Ahem," I said loudly over the laughter. "Is somebody going to clue me in or am I supposed to guess?"

Kimberly drew in long breaths, as if to calm herself from so much hysteria. "It's just that the Angels—" She broke off, dissolving again into laughter.

"We've come up with the way the Angels would define trouble," Lila chimed in through her giggles.

"How's that?" I asked.

"Their idea of getting in trouble is having their library cards taken away for a week," Lila replied, cracking up again.

I giggled softly. Now was definitely not the time to be making Angel jokes—not when I'd just invited Mandy to join us for lunch.

Kimberly took a sip of orange juice, then began to

giggle again. "And did you see the way Evie—"

"That's a great sweater, Kimberly," I broke in quickly. "Is it new?"

"This?" Kimberly glanced down at her sweater, then gave me a funny look. "I've had this forever. You've seen it about a hundred times."

"I have? Oh, yeah, I guess now that you mention it, I have," I told her. "Well, it looks really good on you."

Kimberly smiled and pushed a few strands of hair behind her ear. "Thank you, Jessica. Speaking of clothes, my mom said she'd take me to the mall this afternoon. She wants to buy me a new outfit to try and cheer me up about the election."

"Cool," Ellen said. "What do you think you're going to get?"

"I have my eye on this adorable little black dress that would look great with my cowboy boots," Kimberly said. "So maybe I won't be student council president, but at least I'll look good."

"Did you tell your mom about the speech and everything?" I asked.

Kimberly frowned. "No, of course not. That speech is totally beside the point anyway, don't you think?"

I bit my lip. "Well, yeah, I guess, but—"

"The point is that everyone knows I'm a hundred times more popular than little Mary Wallace," Kimberly continued. "If that goody-goody Mandy hadn't told on me about the speech, I would be the president of the student council—right where I belong."

Great timing. At that exact moment, Mandy walked away from the cafeteria cashier and headed toward our table. *Please keep walking and go right past us*, I begged her silently. This was obviously not the time to try to get the Unicorns to make peace with Mandy.

"Everyone thinks she's such a little saint just because she was sick," Kimberly went on.

I shot her a look. "That's a rotten thing to say," I blurted out. You see, Mandy had cancer last year. She's OK now, but it was really scary at the time. I could put up with a lot from Kimberly, but no way was I going to let her pick on Mandy like that.

"Lighten up, Jessica," Lila said, flipping her long brown hair over her shoulder. "She's only joking."

"Well, I don't really think that's something to joke about," I said.

"What isn't something to joke about?" Mandy asked. She was standing behind Ellen and Kimberly, holding her tray and smiling hopefully.

"Hi, Mandy," I said excitedly, even though I felt like I had a big pit in my stomach. "We were just saying that that big term paper we have to write for social studies class is nothing to joke about."

"Oh, right. It should be a killer." Mandy set down her tray and took a seat between Ellen and Lila. "Sorry it took me so long," she said. "I guess they had to fly back to Italy to make a new batch of lasagna."

"Maybe you should fly there with them and give them a hand," Kimberly muttered in her I'm-going-to-pretend-I-don't-want-you-to-hear-me-but-I-really-do voice. "This school could stand to lose a traitor."

Suddenly I wanted to crawl under the table. Mandy went pale.

"Gee, Jessica," Mandy said through gritted teeth, "I guess this was just another little prank you were playing. 'Let's make Mandy think we want her to sit with us and then when she joins us we'll be really nasty.'"

"No, that's not true," I protested, feeling my cheeks grow warm. "I really did want you to sit with us."

"Yeah, right," Mandy said sarcastically. "And the new president of the student council is Kimberly Haver." Mandy stood up and headed straight toward the table where Elizabeth was sitting with the other Angels.

I looked across our table at Kimberly, who was glaring at me.

"What was the point of that little invitation?" Kimberly asked me.

I sighed heavily. "I guess I thought it would be nice to make peace with Mandy."

Kimberly rolled her eyes. "That's funny—the last time I checked, Mandy was an Angel."

"Kimberly's right," Ellen piped in. "We really shouldn't socialize with Angels."

That was typical Ellen. She's a great girl and everything, but she's not exactly what you'd call an individual thinker. She usually just goes along with the crowd.

"I think you should get your priorities straight," Lila said. "Your loyalty has to be to the Unicorns."

"My loyalty *is* to the Unicorns," I insisted. "I mean, I'm sitting with you guys, right? I just thought—"

"We know what you thought, Jessica," Kimberly interrupted, "and you can forget about it. You're a Unicorn and Mandy's an Angel, and the two groups don't mix."

"Well, I see what you mean, but maybe—"

Lila put her arm around my shoulder. "Come on, Jessica, where's your Unicorn spirit? Don't you remember how much fun the club used to be before we let in those goody two-shoes? I mean, all we cared about was being the prettiest, most popular girls in Sweet Valley Middle School. None of this save-the-world business."

"She's right, Jessica," Kimberly said. "I mean, how can we call ourselves an exclusive club if we let in just anyone?"

"Well, yes, but Mandy's not exactly any—"

"Mandy's an Angel," Ellen said, pointing across the lunchroom. "Check it out!"

I looked over at the Angels' table. At that moment, Elizabeth was holding up a pink T-shirt that said *Angels* on the back and *Mandy* on the front. Mandy, Elizabeth, Maria, Evie, and Mary were all smiling and laughing. I felt my stomach knot.

"Yep," Kimberly said, dusting off her hands. "It looks like Little Miss Traitor has finally made it official. She's an Angel all the way. So what do you think now, Jessica?"

I pried my eyes away from Mandy and the Angels. There was only one thing I *could* think. Mandy was obviously overjoyed to be an Angel. Well, if that was the way she wanted it, fine. It's not like I didn't try.

I looked at my friends and held up my carton of milk. "Here's to the Unicorns!"

Two

"These shirts are totally fantastic," Mandy said, holding up her new pink Angels T-shirt.

"You'll be beautiful in it," Mary told her. "I bet the Unicorns will be green with envy."

"Or purple with jealousy," Evie added, referring to the official color of the Unicorn Club.

It was Friday and I was sitting with the other Angels in the school cafeteria at a special table we call the Angeliner. I'm Elizabeth Wakefield, and the Angels are half of what used to be the Unicorns. Well, actually, the Unicorns still exist, but we're not part of them anymore. We decided that our club's goal is to bring out the best in one another. The goal of the Unicorns, on the other hand, seems to be to bring out the snobbiest and most superficial aspects of its members.

Actually, when we were all Unicorns, we were more like the Angels are now. That was until

Kimberly Haver came back to Sweet Valley and the Unicorns started acting the way they did last year, when all they seemed to care about was clothes and gossip and boys and boys and boys. Did I mention they were interested in boys?

But enough about the Unicorns. I smiled at my friends. "Let's wear our new shirts tonight," I suggested.

"That's a great idea," Mary said as she plunged her fork into her lasagna. "We should take a picture of all of us wearing them."

"What time do you want us to come over?" Maria asked me.

"How about seven o'clock?" I suggested. "That will give us time to stop by the day-care center."

We were having our first Angels slumber party at my house that night and everyone was really psyched. It would give us a chance to make plans for our future as a group and spend some time together just hanging out and having fun.

I was also thinking that the slumber party would be the perfect time to mention that I wanted to be president of the Angels. I had all kinds of great ideas about things we could do to make our club even better. In addition to working at the day-care center, I thought we could volunteer at a soup kitchen or something. I also had an idea about starting a book club.

"The party should be a blast," Mandy said. "Will Steven and some of his cute friends be there, by any chance?"

I wrinkled my nose. "Ick. Are you talking about Steven *Wakefield,* my *brother?*"

Mandy giggled. "You have to admit he's absolutely adorable."

"Do I really *have* to?" I teased. "Besides, you're probably out of luck. If he doesn't have a date, I'm sure he'll make one as soon as he finds out we're having a slumber party."

Steven's a sophomore at Sweet Valley High and he's one of the top basketball players there. For some bizarre reason, my friends have always had little crushes on him and his friends. OK, Steven's not really *that* bad—but I wouldn't exactly call him adorable, especially when he gets into one of his bratty moods.

"Oh, well," Mandy said. "Will, um . . ." She looked down at her tray. "Will your sister be there?"

I took a deep breath. "I'm not really sure. We haven't—I guess we haven't been talking all that much lately. I don't know what her plans are."

"Maybe she and Kimberly will be out stealing something tonight," Mary muttered.

I felt my face heat up. Sure, Jessica and I hadn't been getting along all that great lately, but I hated hearing anyone attack her. "That's not a very nice thing to say," I told Mary. "I mean, my sister's not a thief or anything."

"Excuse me, but she *was* involved in that whole speech thing," Mary said, buttering her roll.

"Well, yes, but it's not like she steals things on a regular basis," I pointed out. "And anyway, Kimberly's the one who actually took the speech, not Jessica."

"In my opinion, all of the Unicorns, including Jessica, are guilty," Mary said.

"Look, you guys, do we really have to fight about the Unicorns?" Evie cut in. "We've already had enough conversations about what happened with the election."

I sighed. "You're right. We have better things to talk about—like what we're going to do tonight."

Mary brightened. "I was thinking about maybe going over some ideas I had for the student council."

Mandy raised her eyebrows. "You want to talk about the student council at the *slumber* party? No offense, Mary, but that's not exactly my idea of a great Friday night."

Mary laughed. "Sorry. I guess I'm still so excited about the election and everything."

"Well, it *is* pretty exciting," Maria told her. "Maybe we could squeeze in some student council planning between videos or something."

"Maybe we could do a play reading," I suggested. "I just bought a copy of this famous play by Tennessee Williams called *Cat on a Hot Tin Roof*."

"That's a great idea," Mary said. "And since Jessica won't be there to try to take over the whole thing, we'll all get a chance to play the lead."

Evie, Maria, and Mandy began to laugh. I managed a smile, but I had a weird feeling in my stomach. I couldn't help feeling a little sad that Jessica wouldn't be at the slumber party with us. Of course, she probably *would* insist on playing the lead during the play reading, and she *had* been a major pain lately, but if there was anyone who knew how to make a slumber party fun, it was my twin sister. Besides, she would probably be really hurt when she found out we were having the party at our house and she wasn't invited.

"What's up with *them?*" Maria asked, pointing across the room at the Unicorner.

I looked up and saw what she meant—the Unicorns were laughing hysterically over something. Jessica was laughing the hardest of all. I felt a wave of jealousy. Here I was, feeling bad because the two of us wouldn't be hanging out together that night, and she was over there having the time of her life.

Well, I wasn't going to let her beat me in the good-time department. I gave the Angels my brightest smile. "Tonight we're going to have the best slumber party in the whole history of slumber parties!" I announced.

"OK, news flash," Lila said breathlessly as she came back to the Unicorner. We'd nominated her to be the person to go back through the lunch line to get us all some frozen yogurt.

"Don't tell me they were all out of cappuccino yogurt," Kimberly said, making a face.

"Actually, they were," Lila said. "But that's not the news flash." She set the tray of yogurt on the table, then sat down and leaned forward. The rest of us leaned forward, too, so that our faces were close to hers. "Guess who's having a slumber party tonight?"

"I don't know," Ellen said. "Who?"

"Our *favorite* club of all time," Lila said, looking at each of us meaningfully.

My stomach knotted. "You mean . . ."

"That's right," Lila said, nodding vigorously. "The *Angels* are having a slumber party this very night."

"Oh," I said softly. "I didn't— I mean, Elizabeth never said— Well, she never told me about a slumber party."

"Why would she tell you, Jessica?" Kimberly asked, frowning. "I mean, it's not like the Angels have anything to do with the Unicorns anymore, right?"

"Well, sure. It's just that—"

"Besides, can you imagine how boring an Angels slumber party would be?" Kimberly went on. "They'll probably do their math homework together as one of their big activities. And then for a real special treat, they'll probably work on a science experiment together."

"Then maybe they'll go really wild and bake cookies or something," Ellen added.

"You know, the more I think about it, the more psyched I am that the Unicorns have gone back to the way things were," Lila mused. "After all, we know how to throw a *real* slumber party. In fact, I think we should have one tonight, at my place."

"Excellent idea, Lila," Kimberly said enthusiastically.

"Cool!" Ellen added.

I started to perk up. The Unicorns really *did* know how to throw a slumber party, and slumber parties at Lila's house were the best of all. She lives with her father in a gorgeous mansion on a hill. I absolutely love hanging out in such a luxurious place. Who needed Elizabeth or Mandy or any of the Angels anyway?

Besides, now that Mandy was out of the picture, the Unicorns needed a new president, and I knew just who it should be—me! And what better time to mention that than the slumber party?

"So let's say the slumber party officially begins at around seven," Lila said. "That way we can stop by the day-care center for a while after school. I promised Ellie I'd visit her." Ellie is a little girl at the center. She and Lila are especially close.

"I'm up for going," I added. "I have a book I want to bring to Oliver." Oliver is the little boy I've formed a special bond with. At first we used to fight with each other all the time, but now I feel like he's almost a little brother. "I think he'll be really into this book. It's got these huge, bright pictures of trains and—"

"*Trains?*" Kimberly repeated, cutting me off. "Did you actually say *trains?*"

"Um," I said carefully. Kimberly was looking at me as if I'd lost my mind. "Well, yeah. Trains."

Kimberly shook her head in disbelief, then turned to Lila. "Are you guys serious? You're still thinking of hanging out at that dweeby day-care center?"

Lila blushed and stared down at her frozen yogurt. "It's just that— Well, Ellie kind of expects to see me."

Kimberly frowned. "I thought you guys had gotten all that goody-goody business out of your system. Do you really want to upset the Unicorn image by showing up at that center?"

I took a deep breath. I could sort of see Kimberly's point. After all, last year I definitely would have thought that volunteering at a day-care center was something for super-serious types like my sister. Taking care of kids wasn't exactly a traditional Unicorn activity. But things were a little different now. I really *like* the center, and Kimberly probably would, too, if she'd just give it a chance. "You know, hanging out with the kids is kind of fun," I told Kimberly. "You might even find one or two you especially like."

Kimberly's eyes widened. "I really can't believe you, Jessica Wakefield. I can't believe any of you. Chasing after dirty little children is something the Angels would do. It's definitely not a Unicorn activity. What if the Angels are there this very afternoon? Do you really want to see them?"

"That's a good point," Ellen said slowly. "I mean, we don't want to rub elbows with them if we don't have to."

"No, we most certainly don't," Kimberly said, shaking her head vigorously. She looked from me to Lila. "Do we?"

Lila chewed on her lip. "No. I guess not."

"Jessica?" Kimberly asked me. "You don't especially

want to spend the afternoon with your sister and her little friends, do you?"

"Well, no," I admitted.

"Besides, who wants to mess around with runny noses?" Kimberly continued, twirling her hair with her finger. "That doesn't exactly sound like a Unicorn activity to me."

I squirmed. When she put it that way, the center didn't sound like much fun at all. I didn't like to admit it, but those runny noses and stuff did kind of get to me. I don't really like to get all dirty.

Lila and Ellen were obviously thinking the same thing.

"Yuck," Lila said, shuddering.

Ellen wrinkled her nose. "Ugh."

Kimberly smiled with satisfaction. "See? Aren't you glad that the *real* Unicorns are back now and you won't have to deal with that stuff ever again?"

I swallowed. "*Ever* again?"

Lila laid a hand on my arm. "Well, we don't have to go *today*, anyway."

"Yeah," Ellen added. "Why mess ourselves up right before the slumber party?"

I smiled. "I guess dealing with runny noses and stuff won't exactly get us in the spirit for a true-blue Unicorn slumber party."

"That's the spirit, Jessica!" Kimberly exclaimed.

"But I think you mean a true-purple Unicorn slumber party," Lila added. She seemed to be looking at something across the cafeteria. "By the way, what do you think they're laughing about?"

"Who?" Ellen asked.

"The Angels," Lila said. "They're all cracking up hysterically."

"Who cares?" Kimberly said as she took a spoonful of frozen yogurt. "I'm sure they're laughing about some dumb thing a teacher said in class this morning or something."

Lila laughed loudly. "Yeah, you're right. Definitely. Or else they're making plans for the world's most boring slumber party. Talk about dullsville."

"With a capital *D*," I added, watching the Angels shake with laughter.

Three

When all of us Angels walked into the day-care center on Friday afternoon, I felt as if we were walking into a zoo where all the zookeepers had left the animals alone. Arthur and Oliver were in a screaming fight over a red truck and Ellie was in the corner crying by herself.

Mrs. Willard, the director of the center, rushed over to us. "I'm so glad to see you girls today." She looked totally frazzled. She was holding little Molly in her arms, and Billy was clinging to her right leg.

"What's going on?" I asked Mrs. Willard. "They look like a bunch of Mexican jumping beans."

"They've been bouncing off the walls all day," Mrs. Willard said, pushing a strand of hair from her face. "Maybe you girls can settle them down a bit."

"We'll give it our best shot," Maria said, taking a

deep breath. "But it looks like we really have our work cut out for us."

"Let's organize a game of dodge ball in the backyard," Evie suggested. "Maybe that will help them run off some of that extra energy."

"Good idea," I said. "OK, everyone, let's go outside!" I yelled to the kids. "Last one in the backyard is a rotten egg!"

I felt something pulling on my jacket. I looked down and saw Oliver staring up at me with a tear falling out of one of his big brown eyes.

"Where's Jessica?" he asked. "Arthur took my truck and I want Jessica to get it back for me."

I knelt down and wiped his tear away. "She couldn't come today," I said. "She wanted me to tell you she's sorry, but she had something else she had to do."

It was really funny about Oliver and Jessica. At the beginning they used to fight like cats and dogs. Then they started acting like brother and sister. Believe it or not, they're really pretty similar.

"Where's Lila?" Ellie asked as she came running up to me. "She promised she'd be here today."

I shot a desperate look at Mary. "Lila got kind of busy at the last minute," I told Ellie, grasping at straws. Both she and Oliver looked heartbroken.

Mary frowned. "It's really rotten that the Unicorns would let the kids down like this. I mean, how selfish can they be?"

"Shh." Mandy held a finger in front of her lips.

"Don't say that stuff in front of the kids. There's no reason to get them upset."

"Oh, sorry," Mary said quietly. "I guess I didn't think of that."

"Come on," I said, trying to perk everyone up. "What are we waiting for? Dodge ball calls."

We all filed outside to the backyard. Dodge ball turned out to be the perfect way for the kids to get rid of some of their extra energy. It wasn't the most organized game, but the kids looked like they were having fun. They were all running from one side of the yard to the other even if the ball wasn't being thrown at them.

"Mary was right," Maria said as she walked up to me, dodging the kids. "The Unicorns are being to-tally selfish. I mean, how could Lila break a promise to visit Ellie?"

I nodded. "It's really too bad. Lila and Jessica mean a lot to the kids. Especially to Ellie and Oliver."

"Well, obviously the kids don't mean all that much to *them*," Maria said, rolling her eyes. "And if the Unicorns are really going back to being the snob-biest girls in America, I say the kids don't really need them—no more than *we* do."

I sighed. "No more than we do," I repeated quietly.

"Maybe we shouldn't have ordered these sun-daes." Lila scooped up an enormous spoonful of ice cream with hot fudge and whipped cream. "We need to save room for the big feast I've asked Mrs.

Pervis to get for us tonight," she said, referring to her housekeeper.

It was Friday afternoon and I was sitting at a booth at Casey's with Lila, Kimberly, and Ellen. Casey's is this cool ice cream parlor near our school. It's also a really popular hangout. On this particular day, a group of the cutest guys in school was sitting at the booth right next to us.

"I always have enough room for yummy food," Ellen said, popping her cherry into her mouth.

"Well, you should be careful," Kimberly advised. "You don't want to get fat, you know."

Ellen looked down at her body in alarm. "Are you saying that I'm getting fat?"

"No, I'm just saying you should watch it," Kimberly said, licking the whipped cream off her lips. "It's not a good idea to eat a lot of junk."

"Well, tonight we certainly won't be eating junk," Lila said proudly. "Mrs. Pervis is ordering food from that new gourmet store. I told her we'd want some pasta salads and some good dips for those little tiny crackers. Not to mention those gourmet sandwiches. You know, like sun-dried tomatoes, basil, and mozzarella on focaccia."

"Yum," I said, giggling. That was so Lila. I happen to know that she likes junk food as much as anyone, but her absolute favorite kind of food is the expensive kind. Not that I minded or anything. The food is one of the best things about going over to Lila's mansion.

"Speaking of the slumber party, I know one thing

we can do," Ellen said. "My mom just ordered this really special kind of facial mask that's full of dead minerals from the sea. I thought I'd bring it tonight so we could make ourselves extra beautiful."

"Dead minerals from the sea?" I repeated. "That sounds kind of yucky. Why don't we just go get a bunch of mud from our backyards and rub it on our faces?"

"Actually, sea-mineral masks are wonderful," Lila said authoritatively. "They give your complexion a beautiful, youthful glow. As long as they're the right brand, of course—nothing too cheap."

"Oh, I'm sure my mom's sea-mineral mask isn't at all cheap," Ellen said quickly.

"I hope you'll wash the sea minerals off your faces before tomorrow night," Rick Hunter said, walking over to our table.

Rick Hunter happens to be one of the most adorable guys at our school. He's in the eighth grade and almost every girl has a little crush on him. We were all pretty steamed at him a while ago when he told Mandy that he'd take her to this dance, then changed his mind and asked a girl named Amanda Harmon instead. We got back at him by causing him to mess up royally in a school play. For a while I thought I'd never give him the time of day again, not after what he did to Mandy, but there was no reason to stick up for Mandy anymore—after all, she was an Angel now. Besides, Rick *is* really cute.

"And what's happening tomorrow night?" Kimberly asked, fluttering her eyelashes.

"You're all coming to a party that I'm having at my house," Rick said.

"Ooo, awesome," Ellen said, bouncing a little in her seat.

"Sounds good," Lila said, tossing her hair. "I was just thinking it would be fun to go to a party."

"It's not going to be anything major," Rick said, grinning widely. "Just the coolest party of the whole year. Not to mention the most exclusive. So don't say anything to anyone else about it. I don't want a bunch of geeks showing up at my doorstep."

"Our lips are sealed," Kimberly said, zipping an imaginary zipper over her mouth. "After all, *we* wouldn't want a bunch of geeks showing up at your doorstep, either."

"As members of the Unicorn Club, we *expect* the parties we attend to be exclusive," Lila added.

"What an awesome weekend," Ellen said after Rick was gone. "A slumber party tonight at Lila's and a party tomorrow at Rick's."

"I guess the Unicorns *are* the coolest, hippest, luckiest girls in Sweet Valley," Kimberly said.

"Much cooler than the Angels," Lila said.

"Much," I agreed.

As I walked home from Casey's that day, I thought about what a blast this weekend would be. OK, I admit that not going to the day-care center was bumming me out just a tiny little bit, but I was probably just being silly. I mean, how many girls in Sweet Valley get to go to a totally cool slumber party on one night and to an awesome party full of the cutest guys on the next? Exactly four girls, that's how many—me, Lila, Ellen, and Kimberly.

And speaking of cute guys, Rick Hunter himself rode up beside me on his bicycle at that moment.

"Hey, Wakefield," Rick said, coming to a stop. "You got a minute? There's something I forgot to ask you."

"Sure thing," I told him. My heart started beating fast. Maybe he was about to ask me to be his date at his party.

"Could you tell Elizabeth about my party and tell her to invite Maria and the rest of her friends?" he said.

I stifled a gasp. Elizabeth and the Angels? Was he totally clueless? Hadn't he gotten the word that Elizabeth and her friends were at war with me and my friends? Sometimes guys can be so thick. It took all my energy to flash him a smile. "Of course."

"Great. I'll see you tomorrow night, then," he said as he remounted his bike and rode off.

I continued walking home with a funny feeling in my stomach. I kept thinking of what Kimberly's re-action would be when the Angels showed up at Rick's party—it wouldn't be pretty. And she'd *really* freak if she knew I was the one who had told Elizabeth she was invited.

Then again, chances were she'd never know. And even if she was a little upset about seeing the Angels there, she'd get over it. So what harm would there be in giving Elizabeth Rick's message?

Of course, *I* didn't want the Angels there, either. But Elizabeth would get really upset if she found out I hadn't delivered Rick's invitation.

Not that I cared if she got upset. I didn't. Not at all.

I just thought I should tell her about the party because—well, because.

"Elizabeth, honey, are you sure this is going to be enough food?" my mom asked me on Friday afternoon.

We were in the kitchen unloading groceries for my slumber party that night. When I'd gotten back from the day-care center, Mom had taken me to the store to pick up some snack food. We'd bought cookies, ice cream, chips, and soda.

"This will be plenty," I assured her. "Thanks for taking me shopping. You're the best."

My mom really is the best. Her name is Alice and she looks like an older version of me and Jessica. She's an interior decorator and she loves her job. My dad, Ned, is pretty terrific, too. He's a lawyer and he looks like an older version of my brother, Steven.

"Hey, hands off," I commanded Steven, who was in the kitchen with us, working his way through one of the bags of chips. "Those are for my friends."

"I thought you girls were always on a diet," Steven teased. "I'm just trying to help you out so you won't get fat."

"That's Jessica and the Unicorns you're thinking of," I corrected. "The Angels aren't as hung up on our looks as they are."

"Well, you don't want to get a reputation as the Goodyear Blimps," Steven said.

"Har-dee-har-har," I said, rolling my eyes.

"Your dad and I are going to the Reynoldses' house for dinner tonight," Mom said. "Do you think you should let your friends' parents know that?"

"No, I don't think they'll care," I said. "It's not like you're going to be out all night. Besides, we can all take care of ourselves."

"You're right," Mom said, smiling. "Sometimes I forget that you're not my little girl anymore."

"And little is exactly what she won't be if she polishes off all this food," Steven said, puffing up his cheeks for emphasis.

"That wasn't funny the first time, Steven," I told him. "And it's not any funnier now." But even Steven's obnoxious teasing couldn't put me in a bad mood. Looking at all the food was getting me really excited about my party.

"What's with all the food?" Jessica asked as she breezed into the kitchen. She immediately tore open a bag of cookies and bit into one.

"Didn't you hear?" Steven asked. "Elizabeth and the Angels are having a stuff-your-face-with-junk-food sleepover."

Jessica threw the half-eaten cookie in the sink. She gave me a stare that sent a chill through my whole body.

"*Here*? You're having an Angels sleepover *here*?" She turned to Mom. "Tell her she can't do that, Mom!"

"Calm down, honey," Mom said, looking totally confused.

"Excuse me, but would you mind explaining exactly why I can't have a slumber party with *my* friends in *my* house?" I asked.

"Yeah, what's the big deal?" Steven asked, scratching the top of his head. "You're acting like a deranged weirdo. More so than usual."

Jessica looked at Steven, then at my mom. "Elizabeth *can't* have her party here," she insisted.

"Why not, Jessica?" Mom asked calmly.

"B-b-because . . . because," Jessica stammered. "Well, just because."

"OK, now my sister is acting like a total loon," Steven said.

"It's just not fair," Jessica blurted out. "She can't have a party here with what used to be the Unicorns if I'm not invited. It's not right."

"Mom, could you tell Jessica that's the dumbest thing I ever heard?" I said, feeling my voice shake. "And could you remind her that it's because of the low-down, dirty scheming of the Unicorns that we're not part of the same club anymore?"

"Would you tell my sister that the Unicorns are having a slumber party tonight at Lila's that's going to be the best slumber party in all of history?" Jessica said. "And tell her that the reason it's going to be so good is that there won't be any boring, goody-goody losers there to ruin it!"

Mom put her hand up in the air like a traffic cop. "OK. That's enough. I want this fighting to stop right now. I want you to shake hands and call a truce."

"Oh, please, don't make them do that, Mom," Steven said. "Things were just starting to get exciting. I was about ready to place a bet on who was going to throw the first punch."

"Steven, stay out of this," Jessica snapped. She was fuming so much, I could almost see smoke coming out of her ears.

"Girls?" Mom asked in that impatient tone she uses whenever we fight. "I'm waiting."

Jessica and I just stood there, staring at each other in angry silence.

"Nobody will be going to any slumber party tonight until I see you two shake hands," Mom said sternly. "Or maybe I should say that the two of you will have your own slumber party here together."

That was all it took for us to stick our hands out. We shook for half a second, then dropped hands.

"Truce?" Mom asked.

"Truce," I muttered under my breath.

"Truce," Jessica whispered so softly I could barely hear her.

Four

Well, that settled it. If Elizabeth was going to have the nerve to have a slumber party in my own house and not invite me, then there was no way I was going to tell her that she was invited to Rick's party.

Now, don't get me wrong. It's not like I really wanted to be at a slumber party with the nerds of America or anything. It was the principle of the thing. If you think about it, Mary and Mandy had been part of the original Unicorn Club. Everything would have stayed the same if Maria and Elizabeth hadn't joined up this year. So, really, Elizabeth was pretty much stealing *my* friends away from me. Mary and Mandy would have been going to Lila's party instead of Elizabeth's if things hadn't gotten so twisted around.

If she thought I was going to let her get away

with it, she was forgetting that I am Jessica
Wakefield. I got up from my bed and walked down
the hall to Elizabeth's room.

"Who is it?" she asked after I'd knocked on the
door.

I could tell from her tone that she was still in a
huffy mood.

"It's me," I said sweetly. "Could I come in for a
minute?" Without waiting for a reply, I walked right
in. She was sitting at her desk, writing something in
her notebook.

"What are you working on?" I asked, coming
closer.

"What do you care?" she responded bitterly,
quickly closing her notebook. "And what are you
doing in my room?"

I sighed dramatically. "Look, Elizabeth, this
whole war thing has gotten out of hand."

Elizabeth looked at me suspiciously. "Are you for
real?" she asked, tilting her head to one side.

"Absolutely," I said. "I think Mom's right. I
mean, OK, I wasn't completely sure a little while
ago in the kitchen, but now I want to call a real
truce—and not just because Mom said so."

"Why should I believe you?" she asked.

One annoying thing about my sister is that she's
the most stubborn person in the world.

"You should believe me because I'm your sister,"
I said. Even I had to admit that was pretty lame. It
seemed to work, though. Elizabeth's face relaxed a
little.

"OK, I'll agree to a truce," she said.

"That's great," I said. "Oh, by the way, I have a favor to ask you."

"I should have known this was coming," she said, standing up and pushing back her desk chair. "What do you want?"

I forced a friendly giggle. "I guess you really do know me better than anyone else in the world," I said. "I was wondering if I could borrow something for the party tomorrow night."

"What party?" she asked.

I looked at her as if she must be joking. "Well, Rick's party, of course," I said.

That did it. Elizabeth's face fell.

"You *were* invited to his party, weren't you?" I asked innocently. "It's going to be the best party of the year. *Very* exclusive."

Elizabeth turned her back to me and walked to her closet. "I'm tired of your obnoxious games, Jessica. As I'm sure you already know, I wasn't invited to his stupid party, and no, you *can't* borrow anything to wear."

"Tsk, tsk," I said. "I don't see any reason to be petty about this. I mean, it's not *my* fault you weren't invited."

"Just get out of here," she said, looking through the clothes on the rack.

"Gee, Elizabeth, for someone who's just called a truce with her twin sister, you're not acting very nice," I said. "I'm really sorry you weren't invited. I honestly just assumed you were."

"I think I asked you to get out of my room," she said hotly.

"Very well," I said. "Ta-ta!"

"I'll get it," I yelled to my mom when the door-bell rang later that night. "That must be Kimberly." Her dad was driving us to Lila's for the slumber party. I ran down the stairs and opened the door. It wasn't Kimberly. It was every single goody-goody, traitorous Angel. They were all wearing those stu-pid pink T-shirts with their names on the front and *Angels* on the back.

"Hi, Jessica," Mandy whispered, looking down at her boots.

"Don't tell me," I began. "It's the Girl Scouts sell-ing cookies to raise money for a new set of encyclo-pedias."

"I guess that's supposed to be some kind of funny joke," Mary said to the other girls. "You might want to practice your lines, Jessica. That was pretty lame."

How could she stand in the doorway of *my* house and say that to me? I wanted to slam the door in her face. Lucky for her, Elizabeth walked up at that mo-ment.

"Come on in," Elizabeth said.

"We'd like to, but your sister here is blocking our entry," Mary said.

"Oh, please, come in," I said. "I'm sure you have all kinds of fun little things planned. You might want to get started on your game of pin the tail on the donkey. It'll be your bedtime before you know it."

"Look, Jessica, just cut it with the nasty comments," Mandy said. "We're all just as uncomfortable about this as you are."

I looked hard at Mandy. How could we have gone from being such close friends to total enemies in just a matter of days? Somehow, out of all the Angels, seeing Mandy there hurt the most—but I wasn't about to let her or any of the others know that. After all, it had been her decision to abandon the Unicorns, and from the way she'd looked in the cafeteria earlier that day, she was pretty thrilled with her decision.

"You know something?" I asked in a syrupy voice. "I really don't feel uncomfortable. I'm glad you're having your little party. I'm going to a slumber party at Lila's mansion and I'm sure it's going to be about a zillion times more fun than yours."

"Come on, Jessica," Elizabeth said. "Why don't you just quit while you're behind?"

Just as I was about to say something nasty back to Elizabeth, Kimberly walked up the front steps.

"What have we here?" Kimberly asked. "Are the Angels of Nerdville having a little meeting? Oh, and isn't that sweet—they're all wearing those adorable little T-shirts. They even have their names on them. I think I had a shirt with my name on it like that when I was about eight years old."

"Don't be mean to the poor dears," I said. "They

didn't get invited to Rick's party, so they're feeling a little sad."

"What party?" Mandy asked, her face darkening at the mention of her ex-boyfriend.

"Oh, you don't know about Rick's party?" Kimberly asked, shaking her head sympathetically. "I guess it makes sense that you wouldn't. He did say to us Unicorns that it was *very* exclusive, didn't he, Jessica?"

"Yes, he did," I replied. "In fact, I seem to recall his exact words were something like, 'Don't tell anyone about it. I don't want a bunch of geeks showing up at my doorstep.'"

"Obviously he was talking about the Angels," Kimberly said. "I mean, nobody's geekier than they are. How sad."

"I'm sure Rick wouldn't have a party and not invite me," Mandy said defiantly. "I mean, we're pretty close friends now."

"Well, I guess you're wrong," Kimberly said. "Maybe you don't know Rick as well as you think you do."

"We don't even know if they're telling the truth," Maria said to Mandy. "I mean, let's not forget who we're dealing with here."

"Maria's right," Mary said. "These are the Unicorns. Also known as liars and thieves."

I felt my blood pressure starting to rise. "Why are we wasting our time with these social outcasts?" I asked Kimberly. "We have the coolest slumber party of the century to go to."

"Good point," Kimberly said. "Let's get out of here before I fall asleep from being with so many boring people."

"Have fun," Mary called out as Kimberly and I walked down the front path, and all the Angels erupted in giggles. I remembered how Steven thinks the sound of giggling girls is the most annoying sound in the world. Suddenly I could see his point.

"Who wants another slice of pizza?" I asked my friends. We were sitting around the family room in our house a couple of hours later.

"If I have one more piece, you're going to have to get a helicopter to lift me out of here," Evie said.

"You and me both," Mary said, patting her stomach.

We *had* managed to put down a large amount of pizza in a short amount of time. There were four large pizza cartons strewn around the room and the same number of empty chip bags.

"Now that you mention it, I *am* feeling a little sick to my stomach," I said.

"Me, too," Mandy said with a sigh. "Only, I don't know if it's the pizza or our lovely little exchange with the Unicorns from Nightmareville."

"That was pretty nasty," Maria agreed. "When Jessica and Kimberly get together, it's a good idea to stay as far away as possible."

"I can't believe they'd stoop to lying about Rick's party," Mandy said, shaking her head.

"Really," Mary said. "How stupid do they think

we are? I mean, if Rick were having a party, we'd have heard about it by now."

Evie squirmed. "Um, you guys?"

"Yeah?" I asked her.

"Um, well, I didn't want to say anything, but I think it's true," she said timidly. "Rick is throwing a party."

Mandy looked a little pale. "He— What makes you think that?"

"I went to the mall today after we left the day-care center and I overheard Kimberly talking to her mom in the dressing room at Verve," Evie said. "She was saying that she could wear what-ever it was she was trying on to Rick's party to-morrow night."

"Oh," Mandy said softly.

"She didn't know I was there, and I sort of doubt she'd say that to her mother if it weren't true," Evie continued.

A silence hung over the room for a brief moment.

"Look, let's just forget about that dumb party," I said. "Would we really want to be there if the Unicorns were there?"

"No way," Maria said, shaking her head defi-antly.

"Not me, that's for sure," Mary added.

"A whole night with the Unicorns—yuck," Evie said.

The color was starting to return to Mandy's face. "Yeah, now that I think about it, that's one party I wouldn't go to if you paid me!"

"Great—we all agree," I said brightly. "So let's start the play reading!"

We sat in a circle on the floor. I handed out photocopies of *Cat on a Hot Tin Roof* that I'd made at the *Gazette* office earlier that day. I thought that after the reading, I'd read the list I'd made that afternoon of my ideas for the club. Jessica had walked in on me while I was working on it, so it wasn't completely finished. But I was pretty sure I had most of the ideas in my head.

"I saw this movie on video with my grandmother," Evie said. "It was great. Elizabeth Taylor and Paul Newman were in it."

"Can I read the Elizabeth Taylor part?" Mandy asked.

"Sure. Her name is Maggie," I said. "And then we can all take turns doing it, because it's a juicy part. We have to use a strong southern accent."

"That won't be a problem, dahling," Mary said in a terrible southern accent. "I just *love* talkin' southern."

"Ugh," Mandy said, and we all burst into laughter.

"You should have seen the look on Mandy's face when we told her about Rick's party," I said to Lila and Ellen.

"She looked as if her best friend had been run over by a truck," Kimberly added, giggling.

We were all sitting around Lila's enormous basement after eating a huge gourmet feast. Even though our run-in with the Angels had lasted only a few seconds, we'd managed to get laughs out of it for about an hour.

"Maria looked totally ridiculous, standing there trying to say something mean and funny," Kimberly went on. "I swear, she's got to be the nerdiest girl in our school. I don't see how she *ever* got it into her head that she could be a Unicorn."

"Yeah, I don't know what we were thinking, letting her join," Lila said. "Fortunately, we've come to our senses. I mean, she's *so* uptight. And have you ever noticed the way she walks?" Lila stood up and demonstrated. She put a book on her head and walked in short little prim steps.

"Oh, my gosh, that's *total* Maria!" I exclaimed. "I think that's the best acting you've ever done, Lila."

We all clapped and Lila took a bow.

"Your sister's pretty uptight herself, Jessica," Kimberly said. "Did you ever notice that look she gets on her face when she's all hot and bothered about something?" Kimberly stood up and scrunched up her face like an old, bossy woman. She started waving her finger in the air and walking around the room.

I felt my face heat up. "Actually, I don't think that looks like Elizabeth at all. I think you have her confused with someone else."

"Oh, come on, Jessica," Lila said. "Kimberly's got Elizabeth down perfectly. It's totally obvious."

"Yeah, well," I said, suddenly standing up. "Do you guys mind if I change the CD?"

"Whoops, looks like I hit a soft spot," Kimberly said, putting her hand over her mouth.

"No, that's not it," I said, looking through Lila's enormous CD collection. "It's just that—I'm just afraid that if I laugh any more, my stomach might split in two."

I flipped through a whole row of CDs, but I wasn't really paying attention to them. The truth was, Kimberly *had* done a pretty good imitation of Elizabeth, but that wasn't the point. The point was, no one had a right to make fun of my sister but me.

But now that Kimberly had made that Elizabeth face, I couldn't get it out of my mind. That was how Elizabeth looked when she was upset, all right—like when I'd told her about Rick's party, for instance.

All of a sudden, I felt the teensiest pang of my least favorite emotion—guilt.

Five

"She is dead," I said.

"She is dead," all the Angels repeated.

"She is as light as a feather," I said.

"She is as light as a feather," they repeated.

We were playing levitation in our family room and Maria was our victim. In case you've never played this game, the way it works is that one person lies on the floor while the rest of the group sits around in a circle with their fingers placed underneath the victim's body. You make up a whole story about how the person was in an accident or something, and then on the count of three, everyone lifts the person up. The idea is that the person suddenly becomes weightless, so it doesn't take much effort to lift them.

I don't know how it works exactly, but all the times I've played it, the person usually *does* become weightless. Neat, huh?

At least, I used to think so. For some reason, the game seemed a little boring. I guess it had suddenly hit me that I've been doing levitations for years at slumber parties. I knew there had to be a lot of fun stuff to do, but somehow I couldn't think of anything.

I wondered what the Unicorns were doing at their slumber party. Probably not levitations . . .

"Elizabeth, it's time to count to three," Evie whispered to me, snapping me out of my thoughts.

"Oh, sorry," I said. "OK, on the count of three we will all lift her up. One . . . two . . . three."

"How much pizza did you eat, Maria?" Mandy asked.

Mandy had a point. Maria wasn't exactly as light as a feather. In fact, she was as heavy as a bus. We couldn't even lift her a centimeter above the ground.

"Maria? Maria, are you OK?" Mary asked.

"It looks like she's sound asleep," Mandy said.

"Actually, I'm pretty beat, too," Evie said, covering her mouth as she yawned. "What time is it?"

"It's only nine-thirty," I said. "But I'm tired, too. Maybe it's all that food we ate."

Evie laughed. "What would the Unicorns think if they knew we were falling asleep before ten o'clock?"

"If Jessica were here, she'd have us dancing at full speed by now," Mary said. "She loves to have dance contests at slumber parties. She always makes everyone dance."

"Well, good thing she's not here, or we'd *really* be exhausted," Evie said.

"Yeah. Good thing," Mandy echoed.

"Definitely. I mean, if she were here, we'd be pretty much dead by now," I added as Maria began to snore.

"Tomorrow night's going to be a blast," Kimberly said, squirming in her sleeping bag.

We were all lying around Lila's bedroom. I was holding my eyes open with my fingers so that I wouldn't fall asleep. For some weird reason, I was totally exhausted. Maybe it was from all the dancing I'd done earlier, during our dance contest. Kimberly had acted as if she was the winner, even though I knew for a fact that I was the best dancer.

"I wonder if Aaron's going to be there," I said. Aaron Dallas was my sort-of boyfriend in sixth grade, and I still kind of like him.

"I'm sure he will be," Ellen said. "I mean, he *is* one of the most popular guys in school."

"I bet Rick will ask me to dance," Kimberly said dreamily. "He's a great dancer, and as we all know, so am I."

"Modest," I muttered into my pillow.

"I hope Ken Matthews will be there," Ellen said. "I think he's my new crush."

"Well, I can't even think about the guys who'll be at the party until I know what to wear," Lila said, frowning in distress. "I was looking through my closet earlier, and I couldn't find a thing."

"Oh, *please*," I burst out. "You've got to be kidding."

Lila glared at me. "Why would I be kidding?"

"Give me a break, Lila," I said, unable to keep the exasperation out of my voice. "You're the last person in the world who wouldn't have anything to wear. Just walk into your closet. It's three times the size of my bedroom and it's got more clothes in it than all the stores in the mall put together."

Lila's face was completely hard. "*Excusez-moi*, but just because I have a lot of clothes doesn't mean I have everything I want, you know." She sniffed.

"Yeah, well," I began, "I'm just saying you have more clothes than the rest of us."

"Well, I wasn't talking about the rest of you," Lila said huffily. "I was talking about myself."

"So what else is new?" I muttered.

"What?" Lila asked icily.

"Listen, you guys, let's just drop this whole discussion," Kimberly said. "It's getting really old."

"Good idea," I said. "It's wearing me out."

Kimberly frowned. "Jessica, it's not even ten o'clock. Don't tell me you're going to be a party pooper."

"I'm not a party pooper," I insisted. "You were yawning yourself just a few minutes ago, Kimberly."

"We need Mary here to tell one of her famous ghost stories," Lila said. "That would wake us up."

"That's the truth," Ellen said. "I remember one slumber party last year when Mary told a story that was so scary, I couldn't fall asleep all night."

"Do you mean the one about the bloody fingers?" I asked excitedly.

"Exactly," Ellen answered, wide-eyed.

"That was so creepy at the end, when the bloody fingers start moving across the floor and jump up on the girl," I said. "I'm getting scared just thinking about it."

"Well, I'm great at telling ghost stories," Kimberly announced.

"You are?" I asked. I couldn't remember ever hearing her tell a ghost story.

Kimberly shot me a look. "Yes, I am. Much better than Mary, I might add."

"OK, so let's hear it," Lila said. "Tell your story."

"All right. Once there was this girl who lived in Sweet Valley," Kimberly started.

"She can't live in Sweet Valley," Lila said.

"Why not?" Kimberly asked.

"Because that's stupid," I told her.

"Fine. Once there was a girl who lived in New York City," Kimberly continued. "She was very rich and lived in a penthouse apartment that overlooked the whole city."

"What was her name?" I asked.

"Uh . . . Stephanie," Kimberly said. "Anyway, one day Stephanie was all alone in the penthouse when she heard a noise at the window."

"What kind of noise?" Lila asked.

Kimberly sighed. "A tapping noise," she said impatiently. "Now, would you guys stop interrupting me?"

"Sorry," Lila said, looking at me. We both suppressed giggles.

"Anyway, she heard this noise at the window and walked slowly toward it," Kimberly said, trying to sound scary.

"And then what happened?" I asked. Somehow I just *had* to irritate her.

Kimberly darted a harsh glance my way. "She pulled open the curtains and saw a shadowy figure moving around. . . ."

I burrowed down deeper in my sleeping bag. I was becoming sleepier and sleepier.

When I woke up Saturday morning in my sleeping bag I felt like I'd been run over by a truck. I was so tired, it seemed as though I'd hardly slept. When I swallowed, my throat felt like it was on fire. I tiptoed across the family room to the downstairs bathroom, trying not to wake any of the Angels.

When I looked in the mirror, I shrieked. There were tiny little red spots all over my face.

"What's wrong?" Maria asked as she flung open the door.

I looked at her for a second, speechless. "Spots! You have them, too!" I finally told her. "Look in the mirror!"

One by one, all the Angels came running into my bathroom. And one by one, everyone looked in the mirror and saw that they also had red dots all over their faces.

"What's wrong with us?" Maria cried. "Do you think it's the chicken pox?"

"I've already had the chicken pox," Mary said.

"Me, too," Mandy gasped.

"Maybe it was the pizza we ate," Evie suggested.

"Maybe it's a bad case of acne," Mary said. "We did eat a lot of chocolate last night."

"How can you joke about something like this?" Maria asked in a panicked voice.

"I'm not joking," Mary said. "I just think we should try to remain calm and think about what might be wrong."

"What's going on?" my mom asked as she came flying through the door.

There were so many people in the bathroom at this point, we could barely move.

Mom looked at our faces and shook her head knowingly. "German measles," she said. "I had the same thing when I was your age."

"Is it serious?" I asked, looking back in the mirror at my spotted face.

"Not really," Mom said. "I'm going to go call the doctor and see what he says we should do. In the meantime, I'll have your father make you some breakfast."

"German measles!" we all cried in unison as my mom left the room. Even though it wasn't that funny, we all burst into hysterical laughter. We did look pretty ridiculous.

I sat up in my sleeping bag Saturday morning in Lila's basement and stretched my arms. My neck and shoulders were extra stiff, so I rotated my head.

I thought everyone else was asleep until I saw Kimberly start to move.

"Oh, my gosh! Your face!" I gasped when she sat up and looked at me. Kimberly had little red dots all over her face.

"*My* face? *Your* face is the one that has a bad case of acne," Kimberly said. "You might want to consider not going to Rick's party tonight."

"Kimberly, you're the one with dots all over your face," I said.

By this time everyone else was awake and shrieking at each other. You see, we were all covered in dots!

"OK, girls," Mom said as she walked into the kitchen. "I've got some good news and some bad news."

We were all sitting around the table, eating the pancakes my dad had made. We kept looking at each other and giggling. It was just too funny to see each other covered in spots.

"What's the bad news?" I asked.

"Well, I talked to Mr. Fowler, and it seems that all the Unicorns have the German measles," Mom said.

"That's more like the good news," Mary said with a giggle.

"Also, Mrs. Willard called to say that some of the kids at the day-care center are sick with the German measles, too," Mom continued. "That's probably how you all got them."

"Poor kids," Mandy said sympathetically. "So what's the good news?"

"I talked to the doctor and he said it definitely sounds like the German measles," Mom said. "It's not very serious, but you shouldn't be around other people for a couple of days."

"How is that good news?" I asked, imagining myself cooped up in my room all alone.

"You all have to stay together," Mom explained. "The doctor doesn't want you girls to infect your siblings, so you'll all stay here till you're no longer contagious. That means your slumber party can continue for a couple more days."

"Yippee!" Maria yelled. "A marathon slumber party!"

"We don't want you girls to do anything too rambunctious," Dad said. "But you can still have fun. If you'll give me a list of movies you want to see, I'll drive down to the video store and rent them for you."

"That would be great, Dad," I said, starting to give him a hug. I stopped right before I put my arms around him. "Whoops, I guess I shouldn't get too close. I don't want to give you the German measles."

"I'd say we pretty much lucked out getting the measles," Evie said. "All we have to do is hang out together watching movies, eating yummy food, and playing games."

I raised my glass of orange juice. "Here's to the German measles," I said as we all clinked our juice glasses together.

Six

"So are you saying that we have to stay by ourselves for the rest of the weekend?" Lila asked her father incredulously.

We were sitting around Lila's dining room table on Saturday morning, eating strawberry waffles. Mr. Fowler had just come in the room to tell us what the doctor had said to him on the phone.

"Actually, you'll all be quarantined here," Mr. Fowler explained. "Think of it as an extended slumber party."

"All right!" Ellen exclaimed. "That's the coolest—What?" She broke off when she saw Lila staring at her. Lila and Kimberly had both turned a funny color, and I don't think it was because of the German measles. I think they were thinking the same thing I was thinking—if we were all stuck at Lila's, we couldn't go to Rick's party.

Suddenly Lila looked at her father with her most innocent expression (which doesn't come close to being as convincing as mine). "Dad, if we take it really easy all day, and we're feeling a hundred times better tonight, do you think we could go to Rick's party?"

Mr. Fowler smiled and shook his head. "N-O. No. Absolutely not."

"But if we feel so much better and our spots are completely gone?" Lila pursued sweetly.

"Honey, the doctor said you'll be contagious for at least another twenty-four hours," Mr. Fowler explained. "That's why he wants you all to stay here. He's afraid that if you go back to your homes, you'll give this to your brothers and sisters."

Kimberly let out a heavy sigh. "I can't believe we have to miss Rick's party. I mean, of all weekends to be covered in spots! I wonder how we got these measles."

"Well, I just talked to Mrs. Wakefield, and she told me that Elizabeth and everyone at her slumber party have the same thing," Mr. Fowler explained. "Apparently some kids at the day-care center also have it."

"Great," Kimberly said, looking annoyed. "You'd almost think those Angels were trying to ruin our lives on purpose."

Lila gave me a sideways glance. "I guess Elizabeth gave it to Jessica and she gave it to us."

"That reminds me," Mr. Fowler said, putting his index finger on his forehead. "Jessica, since Elizabeth has the same thing, you should feel free to go home if you'd prefer to convalesce there."

Before I could answer, Lila turned to her dad in horror. "Are you *kidding?*"

"Why would she punish herself by spending time with the Angels?" Kimberly asked.

"They're right, Mr. Fowler," I said quickly. "I wouldn't go to the Angels' slumber party if I were on my deathbed."

"Whatever you like," Mr. Fowler said, walking out of the kitchen. "Well, try to have fun, girls. Holler if you need anything."

"You know, in some ways, getting these German measles might be the best thing that could have happened," Kimberly said when Mr. Fowler had left the room. "I mean, now none of us will have to see a single Angel for at least twenty-four hours."

"Good point," I said. "And we'll definitely have a lot more fun at our slumber party than the Angels will at theirs."

"That's for sure," Ellen agreed.

"Let's think of all the things we can do today," Lila said.

"We could have another dance contest," I suggested.

"I don't know about the rest of you, but I think I'm a little too tired for dancing," Kimberly said.

"Me, too," Lila said. "I'm kind of low on energy."

"Well, we still haven't done those facial masks I told you about," Ellen said.

"That's probably not a good idea," Kimberly said.

"I mean, it might not be good for our spots."

"Oh, my gosh," I exclaimed, putting both hands in front of my face and cracking up.

"What's wrong?" Lila asked.

"I'd almost forgotten about your spots until Kimberly just said that," I said, trying to hold back a laugh. "You guys look like you just had a red jelly bean fight and all the beans got stuck on your faces!"

"Excuse me, Miss Cherry Pie Face, but you seem to have forgotten that you have the same beautiful spots we do," Lila said, putting her hands on her hips.

"Yeah, you're right!" I said, covering my face with my hands and laughing through my fingers.

Everyone else started laughing hysterically, too.

"Hey, let's give ourselves makeovers," Lila suggested once her laughter had subsided. "Not our faces, but our clothes and hair. We can go into my closet and try on all my stuff and make up new outfits."

"Too bad Mandy isn't here," I said. "I mean, making up funky outfits is her specialty."

"I'm sure we're perfectly capable of coming up with cool outfits ourselves," Kimberly said haughtily.

I raised an eyebrow. "Well, yeah, but—"

"I mean, Mandy's not the only one who has any fashion sense, you know," Kimberly went on. "Just like Mary's not the only one who knows how to tell a good ghost story."

Lila, Ellen, and I exchanged looks.

"You'd almost think you miss the Angels or something, the way you can't stop talking about them," Kimberly continued.

"That's ridiculous," Lila said. "I don't miss the Angels one single bit."

"I'd rather be alone in my bedroom than spend the day with them," I added.

"Me, too," Lila said.

"Me, three," Ellen chimed in.

"Well, good," Kimberly said, smiling with satisfaction. "Now let's go raid Lila's closet."

"Has that poor coyote ever caught the roadrunner?" Mandy asked.

"What do you mean, *poor* coyote?" Maria asked. "He's the bad guy."

We were watching cartoons in the family room later that morning.

"I guess I just feel bad for the coyote," Mandy said. "I mean, he puts so much effort into catching that roadrunner. He should at least get to catch up with him every now and then."

"You're such a softy," Maria teased. "I suppose you also feel sorry for that cat who never catches the mouse. What are those guys' names?"

"Tom and Jerry," I said. "Let's see if they're on now." I picked up the remote control and channel-surfed.

"Hey, go back to that music video," Evie said. "I love that new song by Christalla."

"Does she have a last name?" Mary asked.

"No, I don't think so," Evie said. "I think she's just Christalla."

"I just thought of something," Mandy said, grinning. "If the Unicorns have the measles, too, they won't be able to go to Rick's party tonight!"

"You're right," Mary said excitedly. "I hadn't thought of that."

"And you just know how much they were looking forward to it," Mandy said. "I'm sure they're royally bummed out right now."

"And let's not forget that we're talking about the four most conceited girls in Sweet Valley," Mary added.

"Good point," Maria said, laughing. "I would love to have been a fly on the wall when they first looked in the mirror."

I laughed, too. It *was* a funny image. The Unicorns are probably the vainest people on the planet.

"Sorry, Jessica, but I just can't do it," Steven said into the phone in the upstairs hallway. "Mom is making me go to Joe's for the rest of the weekend so I don't catch that measles thing."

I was walking up the stairs to get a board game from my room, and I couldn't help overhearing Steven's conversation.

"Besides," he was saying into the phone, "I'm not really in the mood to ruin Elizabeth's party."

I stopped in my tracks. Ruin my party? What was going on?

When Steven hung up the phone, I started walking down the hall.

"OK, what did Jessica tell you to do?" I demanded.

"Whoa, stay away," Steven said, covering his face with his hands. "I don't want those disgusting things you have on your face."

I stopped about ten feet away from him. "I won't come any closer," I said. "And take back what you said about my face being disgusting."

"OK, I take it back," Steven said. "I guess I'm just not used to seeing you in polka dots."

"Whatever," I said. "Now tell me what Jessica just said."

"Why don't we drop it?" Steven said nervously. "It wasn't important."

"Come on," I pleaded. "I know she told you to do something to mess up my party. Just tell me what it was."

Steven sighed. "Look, you know I hate to get in the middle of your and Jessica's stupid fights," he said.

I folded my arms. "You can make an exception this one time. I have a right to know what she was planning to do to my party."

"All right, but don't tell her I told you," Steven said.

"I promise," I said, crossing my heart for extra emphasis.

"Well, it's totally stupid and I'm not doing it," Steven said. "So don't think I had anything to do with it at all."

"OK, OK," I said impatiently. "Just spit it out."

He took a deep breath. "Jessica asked me to get a bunch of bugs from outside and put them in your sleeping bags when you weren't looking. I guess she was hoping you'd all be so freaked out that the party would break up."

My chest tightened. What a totally rotten trick! "Thanks for telling me about her silly scheme, Steven," I told him. "I owe you one."

"No problem," he said. "Now, I'm out of here before I end up with a pizza face."

"You guys aren't going to believe what I'm about to tell you," I said as I bounded back into the family room.

"You got a new spot?" Maria teased.

"It's about the Unicorns," I explained.

"What about them?" Mandy asked, rolling her eyes.

"Jessica just called Steven to try to get him to ruin our party," I said.

"And how was he supposed to do that?" Mary asked.

"That's the dumbest part of all," I continued. "She wanted him to put bugs in our sleeping bags."

"That is so immature," Maria said, laughing. "That sounds like something the guys used to do when we were in third grade."

"You're right," Mandy said between giggles. "I remember walking into my classroom after lunch when I was in third grade and finding out that Joey

Bopper had put a big beetle on my chair."

"Yuck," Evie said, making a face. "Did you sit on it?"

"No. Luckily I noticed it before I sat down," Mandy said. "I thought it was pretty stupid even back then."

"I guess the German measles must be affecting their thinking abilities," I said. "Usually the Unicorns are world-class schemers. Especially my sister."

"That's true," Mandy said, smiling wistfully. "They really know how to get back at someone if they've been double-crossed."

Mary frowned. "You almost sound like you miss them or something."

"Of course I don't miss them," Mandy said quickly.

"Well, good," Mary said. "Because they're not the only ones who are good at getting back at people, you know."

Mandy smiled. "You're right. Certain other people are very good at getting back at people, too. Certain other people known as the Angels."

"So let's outscheme the schemers!" Evie exclaimed.

"What do you think we should do?" I asked.

"We could have tons of really disgusting food delivered to their house," Maria suggested. "And when it got there, they'd be stuck having to pay for it."

"The only problem with that is that Lila's so rich,

she'd just go ahead and pay for it and not think any-thing of it," Mary pointed out.

"We could do a crank call," I suggested.

"Like what?" Mandy asked.

"I don't know," I said. "Maybe like, 'Is Mrs. Wall there? Is Mr. Wall there?'"

"'Then how the heck is your house standing up?'" Maria finished the joke.

"Nice try, Elizabeth, but we've been doing that one since fourth grade," Mandy said.

"OK, what about this one?" I offered, clearing my throat. "'Is your refrigerator running?'"

"'Then you'd better go after it,'" Maria said, giv-ing away the punch line.

Mandy sighed loudly.

"I guess that's been done, too," I said sheepishly.

"Any more big ideas?" Mandy asked teasingly.

"Not really," I said. I had to admit, times like that were when it would have been good to have Jessica around. She *is* the queen of crank calls.

"Let's think about this scientifically," Maria sug-gested, standing up and pacing around the room. "What do the Unicorns care the most about?"

"Boys," Mandy said.

"And their appearance," Mary added.

"I have it," Maria said, snapping her fingers.

"What?" Evie asked.

"Just wait and listen," Maria said. "Elizabeth, can I use your phone? This is going to be the best crank call in all of history." Then she frowned. "Actually, Elizabeth, you should make the call."

"Can you tell me who I'm calling and what I'm saying to whoever it is I'm calling?" I said.

"You're calling Ken Matthews and telling him that you're Jessica," Maria explained. "You're the expert at imitating your sister's voice."

"Fine, but what do I say?" I asked.

"You're going to tell him that you and the Unicorns are hanging out at Lila's and you'd love for him and his friends to come over for an impromptu pool party," Maria said decisively.

"You're a genius," Mandy said, her face lighting up. "Then, when the guys get there, they'll see the Unicorns covered in spots."

"And the Unicorns will be so humiliated that they'll be afraid to show their faces in public ever again," Mary said.

"So what are we waiting for?" Evie asked. "Go for it, Elizabeth."

I drew a deep breath. "I'll admit that it's a good prank. But it seems a little mean."

"And telling your brother to put bugs in our sleeping bags was a *nice* thing to do?" Maria asked incredulously.

"You're right," I agreed. "They *were* trying to mess up our party. The only thing to do is try to mess up theirs."

"That's the spirit," Maria said. "Watch out, Unicorns, because the Angels are on the warpath!"

Seven

"Jessica, can you pass me the tanning lotion?" Lila asked me from her lounge chair.

It was Saturday afternoon, and we'd decided that the sun might be good for getting rid of our spots, so we were hanging out by her pool. As far as I could tell, the sun wasn't really doing much for our spots, but it was making me feel pretty tired and groggy. I couldn't help thinking that usually when I'm sick, my mom and dad fix me special treats. And when Elizabeth and I are sick at the same time, we have a lot of fun playing games and watching movies together. Not that I really wanted to be at home or anything.

"Can you pass the lemonade?" I asked Kimberly. "My throat's kind of dry."

"Kimberly?" I repeated when I didn't get any response.

I looked over at her on her lounge chair and realized she was sound asleep. "I guess sleepiness is one of the symptoms of this measles thing," I said to Lila.

"Do you think so?" Lila asked, yawning.

"Here comes your dad," Ellen said to Lila, looking toward the house. "And he looks pretty steamed."

"Lila, I need to have a word with you and your friends," Mr. Fowler said as he headed toward us.

His tone was so loud and stern that Kimberly woke up and sat up straight on her chair.

"What's wrong, Dad?" Lila asked, looking slightly embarrassed.

"You just had some visitors," he said.

"I did?" Lila asked. "Who was it?"

"Ken Matthews and some other young men said they'd received an invitation to come over here for a pool party," Mr. Fowler said angrily. "Now, you know that you're all here because you're sick and that you're not supposed to be around other people."

"Oh, my gosh!" Kimberly squealed. "We could have been seen like this by those guys!"

I pulled my towel around me. "Total nightmare!"

"I'll say it would be a nightmare," Mr. Fowler said darkly.

"But we didn't call them," Lila protested, looking confused. "I swear, Dad, we—"

"I don't want you to forget that this is *not* a party," Mr. Fowler cut in. "And I don't want to have to force you to stay in bed all day."

"Dad, I promise we didn't call them," Lila said again.

"Well, all I know is that I don't want this kind of thing to happen again," Mr. Fowler said before turning around and walking back toward the house.

"Mr. Fowler?" I asked in my most innocent voice.

"Yes, Jessica?" he asked impatiently, turning around.

"What exactly did you tell the guys?" I asked nervously.

"I just told them you were sick," he answered. "I didn't tell them what you had."

"So you didn't mention anything about our . . . you know . . . spots?" Kimberly said hesitantly.

"No. Not a word," Mr. Fowler said.

"Thanks, Dad," Lila said. "And I'm sorry that whole thing happened, but I really, really swear we didn't call them."

"Well, it's over now," he said. "Oh, and I don't think you girls should stay out in the sun any longer. I don't want you to get overheated." Mr. Fowler walked back in the house.

"What was that all about?" Kimberly asked in her post-nap stupor. "Did you guys call Ken while I was sleeping or something?"

"No!" Lila practically shouted. "We didn't call anyone."

"Well, if you didn't call them, who did?" Kimberly asked.

We looked at one another for a moment. Then, all

at once, we had the same idea. "The Angels!" we shouted in unison.

"I have to say, that seems like a pretty cool prank for an Angel to pull off," Kimberly said, frowning. "I mean, I thought they were too nerdy to think of something like that."

"I guess in all the time they spent with us, something rubbed off on them," Lila said.

"Still, it's pretty weird," I said. "I didn't think they had it in them."

"Me neither," Lila agreed. "That's a prank that's almost worthy of a Unicorn."

"I guess they were trying to get us back for the bug thing," Ellen said.

"Obviously that didn't work or they wouldn't still be together making phone calls," I said, sighing. "That *was* a pretty lame prank we tried to pull. Whose idea was it, anyway?"

"Yours!" Lila, Ellen, and Kimberly said in unison.

"Oh, yeah," I said dismissively. "We're really slipping. I think the Angels have actually outdone us this time."

"I guess they're cooler than we thought," Ellen said.

"Let's not go overboard," Kimberly cautioned. "We *are* talking about the girls from Geekville."

"Good point," I said, then shuddered. "Can you imagine what would have happened if those guys had seen us like this?"

"We're just lucky my dad greeted them at the

door," Lila said. "I hope he wasn't too mean to them."

"Lila, your dad is anything but mean," I pointed out. "You know that better than anyone. He's just mad because he thought you disobeyed him, and he's worried about you because you're sick. Also, he could have told them that we have spots all over our faces, but he didn't."

"Gee, you sound more like Elizabeth than Jessica," Kimberly said a little accusingly. "When did you get to be so understanding and touchy-feely?"

Suddenly I wanted to push Kimberly and her lounge chair into the pool. "You know, Elizabeth might be an Angel, but she's still my sister," I said hotly. "And there's nothing wrong with seeing the good side in someone. That happens to be one of Elizabeth's best qualities."

Kimberly looked at me as though she'd figured out some deep, dark mystery. "Well, well, well, it seems to me that you miss your twin," she said.

"I didn't say that," I snapped. "I'm just saying . . . well, never mind. It's none of your business."

"Elizabeth? Elizabeth? Hello?" Maria was snapping her fingers in my face. "It's your turn. You have a chance to buy Park Place."

"Oh, sorry," I said. "OK, I'll buy Park Place."

We were playing our second game of Monopoly of the day and I was getting a little bored. It's not that I don't like the game or anything; I guess I was just getting tired of feeling as if I had to entertain everyone. Part of me couldn't help wishing I were up in my room reading a book.

"That's great," Mary said. "That's the one you want. Now, if you can get the Boardwalk, you'll be in really good shape."

I stared at her.

"What are you looking at me like that for?" she asked cautiously. "Are my spots looking especially weird or something?"

I shook my head, laughing. "Sorry. I didn't mean to freak you out. It's just that I've never played like this before."

"Like what?" Maria asked.

"Well, whenever I play with Jessica, she's super competitive," I explained. "She would never congratulate me or point out that I had a chance to make a good move if I hadn't noticed it myself." I smiled, looking into the distance. "And the other big difference is that Jessica *always* steals money from the bank."

"That's so rude," Mary commented, rolling the dice. "It must be a relief not to have to worry about people cheating behind your back for a change."

"Huh?" I asked, looking at her. "Oh, right. It *is* a relief. A huge relief."

"That's such typical Unicorn behavior," Maria said, clucking her tongue.

"What do you mean?" I asked.

"Well, if they have it in them to steal, they have it in them to cheat," Maria explained.

"Well, I wouldn't really say *that*," I said, feeling my cheeks flush.

Maria looked at me with surprise. "Say what?"

"Well, that, um, that Jessica's a cheater," I said defensively.

"But you just said it yourself."

"Well, yeah, but . . ." How could I possibly explain that no one had a right to call Jessica a cheater but me?

"You're not suddenly feeling Unicorn sympathies, are you, Elizabeth?" Mary asked me, frowning.

"No, of course not. I just—" I cleared my throat and decided to change the subject. "Speaking of the Unicorns, I wish we could have been there to see Ken and his friends walk in on them."

Maria's face relaxed into a smile. "Yeah, that would have been the coolest."

"I'm sure the Unicorns were totally impressed that we came up with that prank," Mandy said.

"Elizabeth, you were so good at doing Jessica's voice on the phone," Evie said. "For a moment I almost thought it was Jessica."

"Yeah, Elizabeth," Mary agreed. "You're really the one who pulled it off."

"Thanks," I said softly. "I guess I learned a few tricks from Jessica. Not that I think that's a good idea. Learning anything from Jessica, I mean." I cleared my throat again and looked at the Monopoly board. "So let's finish up this great game. Whose turn is it?"

*   *   *

"Who's my next victim?" Ellen asked.

"I guess I'll go next," I said reluctantly.

We were all in Lila's enormous bathroom on Saturday afternoon, trying out new hairdos.

"Don't do anything too radical," I cautioned her as I sat down on a stool in front of the mirror.

"Ellen did a great job on me," Lila said, admiring herself in the mirror. "You have nothing to worry about."

I glanced at Lila. Her hair was in two braids. "No offense, Lila, but I kind of think you look like a little girl," I said. "I mean, you're not exactly eight years old anymore."

Lila frowned. "That's such a rude thing to say, Jessica," she snapped.

"Really, Jessica," Ellen chimed in. "And for your information, braids are in these days. You'd know that if you'd been looking at the fashion magazines."

"For your information, I *have* been looking at fashion magazines," I told her. "I just happen to think the models in the magazines look like they're little girls, too."

Lila applied gloss to her lips. "Well, Jessica, you have no fashion sense."

"Ha!" I laughed. "Everyone knows that I have the best fashion sense in the school—after Mandy, that is."

"Enough about Mandy," Kimberly interrupted. "Jessica, I think you should do something really different with your hair."

I looked in the mirror. "What do you mean? I like my hair the way it is now."

"Well, I'd think you'd want to differentiate yourself from your identical twin," Kimberly said.

"That's a good point," Lila agreed. "Except for the fact that Elizabeth wears barrettes and ponytails all the time, it's really hard to tell you two apart."

"Yeah, Jessica," Ellen said. "Maybe you should do something to establish your own identity."

"I *have* my own identity," I protested. "Anyone who's ever spent any time with us knows that Elizabeth and I are like night and day."

"Well, yeah—on the inside," Kimberly said. "But you can't tell that from looking at you."

"I have just the thing," Lila said, her face lighting up. She bent down and pulled out a little cardboard box from underneath the sink.

"What's that?" I asked suspiciously.

"It's a home permanent kit," Lila said excitedly. "You'll look great with your hair all curly."

Kimberly clapped her hands together. "That's perfect! Then no one will ever get you and Elizabeth confused."

"But I don't want a perm," I protested. "Besides, my mom will be furious."

"It says on the box that the perm will wash out after ten shampoos," Lila pointed out. "It's not like you're changing your hair forever or anything."

"Yeah. So what are you afraid of?" Kimberly asked.

"I'm not afraid," I said, examining my long,

straight hair in the mirror. "It's just that I kind of like my hair the way it is."

"It's not that your hair's not perfectly nice," Kimberly said soothingly. "But I think you'd look extra nice with a perm. Not to mention way different from Elizabeth."

"What if I don't *want* to look way different from Elizabeth?" I asked in frustration. "To you the truth, I *like* having an identical twin. Looking alike is one of the things that makes us so close."

Kimberly frowned. "Don't you mean *were* so close?" she corrected. "Like in the past."

"Really, Jessica," Lila said, applying mascara to her lower lashes. "You'd think that after what she did to you, you wouldn't call yourselves *close*."

"What do you mean?" I asked. "What did she do to me?"

"I mean about the slumber party and everything," Lila explained. "Don't you think having that slumber party at your very own house was a really rude thing to do?"

"Yeah," Kimberly added. "They could have had their party at another Angel's house, but it's pretty clear that Elizabeth wanted it at yours for a reason."

"A reason?" I repeated weakly.

"Think about it, Jessica," Kimberly said, leaning forward. "Your house just happens to be the only house where there's a Unicorn and an Angel living under the same roof. I'd say Elizabeth wanted the party to be there just to hurt your feelings."

My heart shriveled up. It *was* pretty mean of

Elizabeth to hold the Angels' party at our house, of all places.

"So if I were you, I'd want to do everything I could to look different from her," Kimberly continued. "You know—show her you're sick of looking like her."

"And that you've moved on with your life," Lila added.

I looked in the mirror and saw Elizabeth's face looking back at me. We always talked about how much we liked being identical twins. I knew that she'd really be hurt if I changed my hair just so I wouldn't look so much like her. Well, she had hurt me.

Maybe it was time to be a little different from Elizabeth. "OK," I said, shutting my eyes. "You can do it. Make me curly!"

"I look like Shirley Temple!" I shrieked when I took the towel off my head and looked into the mirror.

"Who's Shirley Temple?" Ellen asked.

"She was a child actress in the nineteen thirties," Lila explained calmly. "She had really curly blond hair."

"I think you look adorable," Ellen said, twirling her finger around one of the millions of curly ringlets on my head.

"Totally," Kimberly agreed. "You look cute."

"I don't want to look *cute*," I said, trying to brush out the curls.

"At least you don't look so much like Elizabeth," Kimberly said lightly, playing with the ends of my hair.

I narrowed my eyes. I thought I saw the tiniest hint of a smirk on her face. "Did you guys try to make me look stupid on purpose?" I asked accusingly.

"Oh, come on," Lila said. "We'd never do something like that."

"We keep telling you, Jessica, you look completely gorgeous," Kimberly assured me.

"I look like a poodle!" I burst out.

Kimberly giggled. "I love poodles."

I almost threw my brush at Kimberly's face. "It's not funny, Kimberly!"

"Look, if you wash your hair a lot of times today, I'm sure the curls will go away," Lila said nonchalantly.

"Yeah, and I'm sure that if I wash it enough times, it'll be so dry that it'll just fall out," I said bitterly.

Lila shrugged. "I don't see what the big deal is. It's just hair."

I glared at her in the mirror. "Oh, I can't believe that you of all people are saying that!"

"What's that supposed to mean?" Lila asked, putting her hands on her hips.

"It means that you're about the most conceited person I know when it comes to your hair," I told her.

"Gee, Jessica," Lila said, frowning. "Just because you

look ridiculous, you don't have to take it out on me."

"So now you're saying I look ridiculous?" I cried. "A minute ago you said I was gorgeous."

Lila, Kimberly, and Ellen exchanged looks.

I groaned and buried my face in my hands. "Fine. I'll just wear my hair in a ponytail until these stupid curls disappear."

"That was the most unscary werewolf I've ever seen," Kimberly said later that afternoon. "I've seen dogs that were scarier than that."

We were sprawled out around Lila's basement, and it seemed as if we'd watched about a hundred videos—definitely too much of a good thing. Still, the movies were helping me take my mind off my horrible hair.

"What's the point of that movie, anyway?" Ellen asked, stretching.

"I don't think there was a point," I said. "Unless it was that you shouldn't fall in love with a werewolf."

Lila went over to the VCR and pressed the rewind button. "What movie should we watch next?" she asked.

"I don't care," Ellen said, yawning.

"I think I've seen enough movies to last me till high school," I said, adjusting the couch pillow under my head.

"What else do you want to do?" Kimberly asked.

"I don't know," I said listlessly. "There must be something we haven't done yet."

"We never dressed up with Lila's clothes," Ellen pointed out.

"It just wouldn't be the same without Mandy," I complained.

Kimberly glared at me. "I've already told you, Jessica, I'm sick of hearing about Mandy. I'm every bit as good—"

"Yeah, I know. You're just as great at putting outfits together," I finished for her, rolling my eyes. She was sounding more and more like Janet Howell, our bossy ex-president. "Listen, let's just drop it. I think we're all too tired to get dressed up, anyway." And I was getting tired of Kimberly's acting so snooty. In fact, I was getting tired of her, period.

"We don't feel like doing anything because we've just been lying around all day," Lila said, plopping down on the floor by the television set. "The less you do, the less you feel like doing."

"Is this something you discovered in a scientific experiment, Dr. Fowler?" Kimberly asked.

"It's a proven fact," Lila answered. "But listen." She checked over both shoulders and lowered her voice to a whisper. "I have an idea—something that will wake us up for sure."

"Why are you whispering?" I asked. "Are we going to make a spy movie or something?"

Ellen and Kimberly giggled.

Lila shook her head. "I'm serious, you guys. Here's the thing—my dad is supposed to go on a business trip tonight. You know what that means?"

"It means we get to dress up in *his* clothes, too?"

Ellen guessed. "I hear menswear's coming back into fashion."

"Nope," Lila told her. "It means we're going out."

"And where exactly are we going?" I asked.

"To Rick's party, of course," Lila said, smiling with satisfaction.

I felt my mouth drop open. I was used to Lila coming up with some pretty dumb ideas, but this was one of the dumbest of all time. "First of all, Lila, your dad said we couldn't go, and second of all, we're sick," I reminded her.

"First of all, Jessica, my dad's going out, so he won't know," Lila began. "And second of all, I'm sure we'll feel a lot better if we just get out of the house."

"But we could give these measles to people at the party," I pointed out.

"Jessica, you're starting to sound more like Elizabeth by the minute," Kimberly said, shaking her head. She smiled at Lila. "I think it's a great idea."

"Me, too," Ellen chimed in. "I'm going pretty stir-crazy staying in this house."

"Besides, missing such a cool party would be bad for our reputation," Kimberly added.

I sighed. "Did you guys stop to think for a minute about one minor problem?"

"What's that?" Kimberly asked.

"Just the little matter of the red dots all over our faces," I said. "I mean, you guys might not mind walking into a party looking like an ad for acne medicine, but that's not my idea of making a good impression."

"Oh, that," Lila said dismissively. "No problem. We'll go up to my bathroom and cover our spots with makeup. It'll be easy. They're already starting to fade a little bit."

"I think you need glasses, Lila," I said. "From where I sit, there are hundreds of red dots in this room, and they're all over the faces in front of me."

"Well, they're not as red as they used to be," Lila said. "And I do have top-of-the-line makeup."

"Give me a break," I blurted out. "No makeup in the world could cover up these spots."

"Look, Jessica," Kimberly said with exasperation. "It's pretty clear that you're the only one of us who thinks going to the party is a bad idea, so why don't you just stay behind? I mean, if you don't care how it looks being the only Unicorn *not* going to Rick's party, and if you don't mind hanging out here by yourself while we're all having a blast, and if you—"

"OK, OK!" I broke in. "I'll go—but only if we can cover these spots completely."

"Cool!" Lila exclaimed, jumping up. "Let's go upstairs and get to work. Operation Obliterate Spots is now under way!"

"Elizabeth, are you sure you don't want to cut the tomatoes up into little cubes?" Mandy asked me on Saturday evening.

We were in the kitchen, preparing an elaborate meal for ourselves. Cooking had been my idea—I figured it would be a great way to spend a couple of hours. The only problem was that there were a few too many cooks in the kitchen.

I put my knife down on the cutting board and wiped my forehead off with the back of my hand. "Actually, I think the tomatoes are best like this," I said, picking up a slice and popping it in my mouth for emphasis.

"But when they're in slices like that, they just don't look good," Mandy argued. "Look—I'll show you how much prettier they are when they're in cubes."

Before I could say another word, Mandy picked up the knife I'd been using and proceeded to dice my perfectly cut tomato slices into itty-bitty squares.

Biting my lip, I walked over to the stove to start heating up the skillet for the vegetables. I wasn't about to get all upset over some chopped tomatoes.

"How long should we cook the pasta?" Maria asked, peering at the pot of boiling water on the stove.

"Ten minutes," I answered, reaching into a drawer and taking out a wooden spoon.

"I really think it should cook longer," Mandy argued from across the room. "Like maybe fifteen minutes."

"It'll be all mushy if we cook it that long," I protested.

"Well, it will still be hard if we cook it for ten," Mandy said.

"Let's cook it for twelve and a half minutes," Evie

suggested. She was sitting at the table cutting up the basil.

"That sounds like a good compromise," Mary said.

"Mary, when you're done with the mushrooms, could you start on the onions?" Mandy asked. Actually, it sounded more like a command than a question.

"Sure, no problem," Mary responded.

I started to pour the olive oil in the skillet, but Mandy came rushing over to the stove. "Whoa! That's way too much oil," she said. "We just want to sauté the vegetables lightly. We don't want them swimming in oil."

That did it. I didn't mind getting a few pointers, but it seemed as though Mandy thought she was the authority on everything. "Mandy, why don't you cook the vegetables?" I said, frustrated. "Seems like you're the expert here."

"OK, that's a good idea," Mandy said cheerfully, nudging me out of the way.

I just stood there, amazed, as she stirred the vegetables in the skillet.

After a moment Mandy looked up. "Did you have a question?"

"Um, well, no . . . not really," I said awkwardly.

"Then why don't you go help Evie with the basil?" Mandy suggested.

My eyes widened. Was it me, or was Mandy acting like a drill sergeant? I looked around the kitchen at the other Angels, but no one else seemed to notice she was acting strangely.

"That sauce smells so yummy," Maria said, taking a whiff. "What's the name of this dish again?"

"Pasta primavera," Mandy answered. "Just wait until you taste it." She kissed her fingers like a world-famous chef. "Oh, and that reminds me. While we're on the subject of cooking, I came up with a great idea for the Angels."

"Are you thinking of opening a little Italian café?" Evie guessed.

Mandy laughed. "Not exactly. I was thinking more along the lines of having a bake sale at school."

"And what were you thinking of doing with the money we raise?" I asked as I chopped some basil.

"I thought we could give it to different charities," Mandy said. "Maybe we could give some to the day-care center, too."

"That's a great idea," Mary said enthusiastically.

"Yeah, it really is," I agreed, smiling. I started to feel bad for getting so annoyed with Mandy. Her heart was in the right place.

Mandy stepped away from the stove and made a little bow. "They don't call me club president for nothing."

I nearly dropped the knife on the cutting board. So Mandy just assumed she was president of the Angels? Didn't anyone have anything to say about that?

From the looks of things, no one did. Evie was still cheerfully chopping basil, Maria was keeping an eye on the pasta, and Mary was tearing lettuce for a salad—it was as if they hadn't given the presidency a second thought.

One thing was sure: If I wanted a chance to be president of the Angels, I had to speak up soon.

Eight

"Hold still, Jessica," Lila instructed me as she smeared cover-up on my face.

"I've been holding still for the last twenty minutes," I complained. "This has got to be a record for time spent on making up a face." I looked at the reflection of her bathroom in the mirror. The countertop was completely covered with makeup. "I feel like we've been crammed into this sty for about a year."

"Since when do you care if a room is a little messy?" Kimberly asked incredulously. "You're not exactly famous for your neatness, you know."

"Besides, I don't know where you get the idea that we're *crammed* in here," Lila said, sniffing. "I mean, no one ever complained about the size of my bathroom before."

"Yeah, Jessica," Ellen added. "It seems like you're

just in a bad mood and you're taking it out on Lila's bathroom."

I rolled my eyes. "I'm sorry about insulting your bathroom, which is actually the hugest bathroom I've ever been in. It's just that I'm sick of hanging out in it while you take forever to smear gunk all over my face. I mean, if Mandy were here, we'd have been made up way before now. She *is* an expert makeup artist."

Kimberly threw a hairbrush in the sink. "Are you doing that to annoy me?"

"Doing what?" I asked.

"You know what I'm talking about," Kimberly said through gritted teeth. "I've already told you that I'm sick of hearing about the Angels."

"Can you guys just cut this out?" Lila said. "Jessica, take a look at yourself in the mirror."

I looked in the mirror and almost fainted. My skin was covered in a cakey, orangey mask—everything was covered, that is, except for my spots. Let's just say I looked like—well, I don't know *what* I looked like. I just looked totally ridiculous. Like a sick ghost or something.

"What are you trying to do to me?" I demanded.

"What are you talking about?" Lila asked, brushing a strand of long brown hair away from her face. "I covered your spots. I thought that was the whole point."

"All you did was cover my face in some disgusting foundation that's probably five shades too dark for me," I protested. "My spots are as bright as ever."

Kimberly and Ellen came over to study my face more closely.

"You look fine," Kimberly said. "I think Lila did a really good job. Just relax."

One thing I really can't stand is when people tell me to relax.

"Is everyone going blind here?" I asked with my hands on my hips. "Or do you guys just want me to go to Rick's party looking like—like a swamp creature or something?" I wasn't really sure what a swamp creature looked like, but it's the first thing I thought of.

"Jessica, you're overreacting," Lila said calmly, looking at Kimberly and Ellen. "You look fine. The lighting in here is just really bad."

"She's right," Ellen agreed. "It's way too bright in here."

I took a good look at everyone else's face and realized that they all looked as awful as I did. I also realized that there was no use trying to get them to believe me.

"Lila, can I use your phone?" I asked.

"Sure, you can use the one in my bedroom," Lila answered.

"Who are you calling?" Kimberly asked.

"My mom," I said, even though it was none of her business. "I'm sure she's worried about how I'm doing and everything. I just thought I'd check in."

"How was your dinner, Elizabeth?" my mom asked me that evening.

She and my dad had just come back from a bar-becue. The rest of the Angels were in the family room watching another movie and I had just gone into the kitchen to get us some cookies.

"Great," I said softly. The food *had* been pretty good, but I was still a little upset over how bossy Mandy had been. "Did you have fun at your party?"

"It was really nice," Mom said. "How are you feeling?"

"I'm OK, I guess," I said, shrugging.

Dad put his hand on my shoulder. "You sound tired. I hope you're not overextending yourself by having your friends over."

"Oh, no," I assured him, forcing a laugh. "It's great having everyone here. Absolutely great."

Dad smiled. "Well, I'm glad you're having fun. And you'll be happy to know that your sister's doing better. She called just a minute ago."

"She did?" I asked eagerly. "What did she say? Is she having fun at her party?"

"She said to be sure to tell you that she's having a great time at her party," Dad said.

"Oh," I said flatly. "I mean, that's great." I cleared my throat. "What kinds of things are they doing?"

"She didn't say," Dad answered. "She just said that they've been keeping busy and that she hoped you were having as much fun as she was."

"Oh," I said again, grabbing a plate of cookies. "I definitely am. I'm having the time of my life."

*   *   *

"Dad!" Lila exclaimed.

"Mr. Fowler!" Kimberly and Ellen cried in unison.

"Hi, girls," Mr. Fowler responded. He'd appeared in the doorway of the dining room just as we were finishing up our dinner. I shot a glance at Lila, who was practically choking on her diet Coke.

"I thought you— I mean, shouldn't you be at the airport by now?" Lila sputtered. "Won't you miss your plane?"

Mr. Fowler smiled. "I was about halfway to the airport when I came to my senses. After all, what's more important—a business trip or taking care of my daughter and her friends when they're sick?"

"But—" Lila began. "Well, that's really nice of you, Dad, but you really shouldn't cancel an important business trip on our account. We're OK, really. Aren't we, girls?"

"Getting better all the time," Kimberly said energetically.

"I never felt better," Ellen added, smiling brightly.

"Jessica, too—right, Jess?" Lila asked, looking at me with wide eyes.

"Oh, yeah. Definitely." I suppressed a giggle. It looked like we wouldn't have to make fools of ourselves at Rick's party after all!

"I'm pleased to hear you're all doing so well," Mr. Fowler said.

"See?" Lila said brightly. "You don't have to worry about us. You can still go on your trip."

Mr. Fowler sat down at the table and patted his

daughter's hand. "You don't have to be brave, sweetie. You girls are sick. You deserve to be taken care of. I've already canceled the trip, so we're all set. I even went out and rented you more movies for the night."

"You did?" Lila asked weakly.

"I sure did!" Mr. Fowler said proudly. "I want you girls to be as comfortable as possible while you recover."

"That's really nice of you, Mr. Fowler," I told him, smiling sweetly.

"Yeah," Lila muttered, glaring at me. "Thanks."

"What are you girls doing with all that makeup on your faces?" Mr. Fowler asked, frowning.

"Oh, uh . . ." Lila said nervously.

"We were just playing around with some new makeup techniques we read about in a magazine," I said quickly.

"Well, I think you should take it off," he said. "I doubt it's good for your measles bumps. They'll probably heal faster if they're not all covered up."

"That's a good idea, Dad," Lila said. "We'll wash off our faces right away."

"I'll be in my study if you need anything," he said, leaving the room.

"Great," Kimberly groaned. "So much for going to Rick's party."

"Yeah, it looks like we're trapped," Ellen added.

"Well, at least we have some more movies to watch," I said cheerfully.

Ellen, Lila, and Kimberly looked at me as if I'd

just said I'd robbed a bank or something. "Hey, I just thought we should look at the bright side," I said.

"Can we turn off the TV?" I said later that night. "We've been vegetating for a pretty long time."

"OK. What about reading a story out loud?" Maria suggested.

"Boring," Mandy said, standing up to stretch.

"We could bake some more cookies," Evie suggested.

"I think we've done enough cooking for one night," I said.

"Hey, I have an idea," Mandy said. "At Unicorn parties last year we used to have truth circles."

"That's a great idea," Mary said enthusiastically. "That was so much fun!"

"What's a truth circle?" Evie asked.

"Everyone sits in a circle and you take turns saying something good and bad about each other," Mary explained.

"Something bad?" I repeated. "Isn't that kind of mean?"

"Believe me, it's a fun game," Mary assured me. "Let's just start and Mandy and I will show you as we go along."

"Cool," Evie said. "I love playing games."

"Come on, Elizabeth," Maria said as she and the other Angels formed a circle on the floor.

"Well . . . OK," I said, reluctantly sitting down.

Mandy started writing things down on a piece of paper, then tore the paper into little scraps.

"Now, I'm giving each of you a piece of paper with a name written on it," Mandy said. "When you get the name, start thinking of one good thing about the person and one bad thing."

Mary giggled. "I remember one time last year when Lila left the room sobbing while we were playing this game."

"What did she get upset about?" I asked.

"Janet Howell told her that she was a show-off or something," Mandy said.

I felt a little flutter of anxiety. "I don't want anyone running out of here in tears. Can't we just say *good* things about each other?"

"Don't worry," Mary said casually. "We'll do a mild version."

"I'll go first," Mandy said, clearing her throat. "My person is Maria."

Maria put her hands over her ears and laughed. "I'm not sure I really want you to do me," she said. "Criticism isn't my favorite thing."

"Come on," Mary said. "It's only a game. I'm sure Mandy will go easy."

"Do you want positive or negative first?" Mandy asked.

"Positive," Maria said.

"OK, I think you're really smart, and one of your best qualities is that you're honest," Mandy said. "You're never afraid to say what's on your mind. You don't play games with people."

"Thanks, I like that," Maria said. "Are you sure you don't just want to stop right there?"

"She has to say a negative thing now," Mary said. "That's the rule."

"OK, fire away," Maria said.

"Although I think honesty is a really good quality," Mandy started, "I also think it can be negative."

"Uh-huh," Maria said, crossing her arms in front of her chest.

"Sometimes you come across as a little abrupt, even rude," Mandy continued. "I don't think you even realize it."

Maria opened her mouth, then shut it.

"Remember, Maria, it's only a game," Mary said. "Everyone's going to hear something negative about themselves tonight."

"Of course," Maria said coldly. "I guess I just don't really feel like playing anymore. Elizabeth, can I go upstairs and read in your room?"

"Well, sure, if you want," I said. "But—"

"Don't go," Mandy told her, interrupting me. "You shouldn't be so sensitive. That's just the way the game is played."

"Well, if that's the way the game is played, then I don't want to play it," Maria said. "In fact, if I can be *honest* for a minute, I think this game stinks. I don't see any point in it."

"Maria, wait," I urged.

Maria was already on her way out. "Have fun making each other miserable," she said.

"I didn't realize she was so sensitive," Mandy said after Maria had left the room. "I guess I don't really know her that well."

"That usually happens, remember?" Mary said. "There's always someone who gets their feelings hurt during this game."

"I guess I can kind of see why," Evie said, shifting uncomfortably on the floor.

Mandy smiled at her kindly. "You really shouldn't worry. It's just a game, right? It's fun. Now who wants to go next?"

"Are we sure we really want to keep playing?" I asked. "I don't want everyone to get upset."

"We can't stop now," Mary said. "We just started."

"I'll go now," Evie said. She looked at the scrap of paper in her hand, then crumpled it up. "My person is Mandy."

Mandy looked at her eagerly. "OK, let's hear it. Positive first."

"Hmm," Evie said thoughtfully. "Well, you're cheerful and energetic and you know how to put it to good use."

"Thanks," Mandy said, smiling brightly.

"For instance, there was the time you costumed us all for that movie. We wouldn't have looked so cool and funky if it hadn't been for you," Evie continued.

"Wow, that's such a nice thing to say," Mandy said. "Now, tell me the bad stuff."

"Do I have to?" Evie said. "Can't I just say nice things?"

"Nope," Mary said. "You have to say something negative."

"Go ahead," Mandy said. "I can take it. I'm not hypersensitive, like some people."

"Well, OK," Evie said, taking a deep breath. "I think sometimes you can be a little bossy."

"Bossy?" Mandy asked, scrunching up her face. "Did you just say *bossy?*"

"Uh, yeah," Evie said in a low voice.

Mandy bit her lip. "I've been accused of a lot of things, but never of being bossy."

"I'm sorry," Evie said, looking like she might cry. "I *said* I didn't want to say something negative."

"Do you guys think I'm bossy?" Mandy asked Mary and me.

"Can we just drop this?" I said. "I don't like this game."

"No, I want to know," Mandy persisted. "Do you think I'm bossy?"

I looked toward the door, wishing I could run right through it. "Uh . . . I don't know. I never really thought about it."

"Come on, Elizabeth, just tell me the truth," Mandy pressed. "Am I bossy or not?"

I rubbed my hands together and took a deep breath. "I guess I'd have to agree with Evie," I said. "I don't think you're bossy all the time, but you have been a little bossier than usual lately."

"Well, could you give me an example? When have I been bossy?" Mandy said in a strangely high-pitched voice.

"You know, maybe we should just drop this now," Mary said. "It's kind of getting out of hand."

"No, I want to hear what she has to say," Mandy insisted. "I want examples of when I've been bossy."

"Well, tonight when we were cooking, for example," I said.

"What are you talking about?" Mandy asked, her face turning red.

"You kept telling everyone how things should be done," I explained carefully. "Like that business of how long the pasta should be cooked and how the tomatoes should be cut and—"

"Excuse me, but I'm the one who prepared that entire meal practically by myself," Mandy broke in.

"Please, let's just stop this whole discussion right now," Evie pleaded.

"No, I want to hear more," Mandy said, her back stiff.

"Listen, Mandy, I really didn't mean to upset you," I told her. "Evie's right. We should end this game right now."

"Fine," Mandy said. "I'm glad to know how you really feel about me."

"Mandy, I'm sorry if your feelings are hurt, but it's just a game, remember?" I said.

"Let's forget we ever played it," Mary said, jumping up from the floor. "How about another movie?"

I awoke on Sunday morning to the sound of the phone ringing. I stumbled out of my bedroom into the hallway to answer it. That's right—my bedroom.

I couldn't fall asleep in the family room, so after all the other Angels had nodded off, I crept upstairs to my own comfortable bed.

"Hello?" I said sleepily.

"Elizabeth?"

"Jessica?" I asked excitedly. It seemed like forever since I'd heard her voice. "How are you feeling?"

"Oh, fine," she replied. "I'm having a really fun time here at Lila's. The best. How about you?"

"Oh, me, too," I told her. "A great time."

"Well . . . good," she said, hesitating.

"So, um," I began after a long silence, "so why are you calling?"

"I . . . uh . . . I was wondering if you could do me a favor," she said.

"A favor?" I repeated.

"Yeah, it's really important," she said.

"What?"

"Could you go into our bathroom and see if I left my curling iron on?"

I frowned. "Your curling iron?"

"That's what I said."

"OK, hang on a minute." Sighing, I walked into the bathroom. The curling iron wasn't on—in fact, it wasn't even in the bathroom. I went back into the hallway.

"It's not on," I told her. "Anything else?"

"Uh, yeah, actually," she said. "I also wanted to say that . . . um, well, did I mention what a great time I'm having here?"

"Yes, Jessica, you did," I replied, getting annoyed.

"Did you have anything *else* you wanted to say?"

"Yes. I thought you should know that your stupid prank didn't work," she spat out.

"Too bad," I said. "And while we're on the subject of pranks, *you* should know that *your* stupid prank didn't work, either."

"Too bad," she snapped. "Well, I guess I should go. I have stuff to do."

"Me, too," I told her.

"OK, then," she said.

"OK." My stomach felt hollow. "Bye."

"Bye."

Nine

"Hey, Elizabeth," Maria said when I walked into the family room on Sunday morning. "We were wondering what happened to you."

I smiled and tried to get the irritating phone call I'd just had with Jessica out of my mind. "I couldn't sleep very well last night," I explained. "I was afraid all my tossing and turning might keep the rest of you awake."

Mary sat up in her sleeping bag. "I can't believe we get to spend another whole day together," she said excitedly.

"I know," Evie said, stretching. "I feel like it's my birthday or Christmas or something."

I have to say, I was a little surprised at how cheerful everyone seemed. After all, we hadn't exactly been in the best mood the previous night. "I hope everyone's feeling OK about what happened last night—I mean, with the truth game and every-thing," I said, looking at Mandy.

"I'm OK about it," Mandy said, smiling weakly.

I raised my eyebrows. "Really? Or are you just saying that?"

Mandy drew in a deep breath. "I can't really be mad about it," she said thoughtfully. "For one thing, it was my idea to play the game in the first place, and besides, I had upset Maria right before that. I guess I had it coming. I say we just forget about it."

Wow! She had seemed so upset the night before, I never would have imagined she'd be so level-headed in the morning. "I'm glad you're feeling bet-ter about it," I told her. "How about you, Maria?"

Maria waved her hand in front of her as if she were getting rid of an irritating fly. "I've already for-gotten about it," she said. "But let's never play that stupid game again."

"I second that motion," Mandy said, laughing. "Anyway, that's more of a Unicorn kind of game."

I giggled. "Yeah, you're right." I cleared my throat. "Speaking of Unicorns, I just got off the phone with Jessica."

Mandy hugged her knees against her chest. "Did she call to chew you out about the prank we pulled?"

"Actually," I said slowly, "our plan didn't work. I guess Mr. Fowler turned the guys away at the front door."

"Shoot," Mary said. "We should have thought of that."

"What else did she say?" Evie said. "Did it sound like they were having a good time?"

"Yeah, it did," I said, trying to sound nonchalant.

"Well, I'm sure they're not having as good a time as we are," Maria said, grinning.

"That goes without saying," Mandy added. "The Angels are the ones who know how to have fun."

"Speaking of fun, what do you guys feel like doing today?" Evie asked.

Mandy stood up. "I thought now would be a good time to have a talk about the future of the Angels."

I felt my chest tighten. I had a feeling Mandy wanted to talk about what *she* was going to do as president of the Angels. And if I didn't speak up soon, she was going to start acting like the president. "Um, you guys?" I said timidly.

"Yeah, Elizabeth?" Mandy asked sweetly.

"Well, I was just thinking that, um, well . . ."

"Is something wrong, Elizabeth?" Mary asked, looking concerned.

I bit my lip. We'd all just made up after what had happened the night before, and somehow I couldn't stand the thought of causing any more tension. "Nothing's wrong—I'm just hungry," I told them. "Why don't we have breakfast and get dressed and then maybe later we'll discuss the Angels' future?"

"Sounds good," Mary said. "Let's raid the kitchen!"

"Are there any more jelly doughnuts in that box?" I asked. It was Sunday morning and we were eating doughnuts in our sleeping bags. We'd spent the night in Lila's basement again. Did you know that basement floors in mansions aren't any more comfortable than basement floors in regular houses?

"What about a chocolate one?" Lila offered. "The jellies are all gone."

"OK," I said listlessly as Lila handed me a chocolate doughnut. Besides not having slept too well and the sudden disappearance of the jelly doughnuts, I was bummed over one other thing: my annoying phone conversation with Elizabeth. I mean, did she really have to rub in what a great time she was having with her boring Angel friends?

"So, what do you guys feel like doing today?" Lila asked, finishing up her doughnut. Her jelly doughnut, I might add.

"We could get your dad to rent some more movies," Ellen suggested.

"Oh, that's original," I told her. "Where'd you ever come up with that idea?"

Ellen set down her glass of orange juice. "Well, you don't have to be such a brat about it, Jessica. Do you have any better ideas?"

"Yeah, I do, actually. How about if we play a board game?" I suggested. "Like Monopoly or something."

Kimberly rolled her eyes. "Jessica, maybe you *should* be at the Angels' party. That definitely sounds like their kind of activity."

"What's wrong with playing Monopoly?" I asked defensively.

"It's just so juvenile," Kimberly answered.

I folded my arms. "So what do you want to do that's so mature?" I asked her.

"What about truth or dare?" she suggested.

"Oh, that's really mature," I said sarcastically.

"Let's take a vote," Kimberly said. "Everyone who wants to play truth or dare, raise your right hand."

Of course, everyone raised their hand except me. I say *of course* because more and more it seemed that Kimberly was acting bossier and bossier—and the bossier she was acting, the more the others were following her lead.

"OK, who wants to go first?" Kimberly asked.

"I will," Ellen volunteered.

"Do you want a truth or a dare?" Kimberly asked.

"Sorry, but who put you in charge of the game?" I asked Kimberly.

Kimberly frowned. "You're awfully touchy this morning, Jessica. You can come up with Ellen's truth or dare if you want. We all take turns, anyway."

"Fine," I said. "Ellen, do you want a truth or a dare?"

"A dare," Ellen said. "But don't make it too hard."

"OK," I said, thinking fast. "I dare you to call Rick Hunter."

"And say what?" she asked.

"Say that you're Mandy and that you can't stop thinking about him and that you've never gotten over breaking up with him," I said.

"What if he recognizes my voice?" she asked.

"That's the whole point," I said. "You have to try to sound like Mandy. That's why it's a dare."

Ellen looked around the room nervously. "OK, hand me the phone."

"This is going to be good!" Lila squealed as Ellen dialed his number.

"Hi, Rick," she said into the phone in a nasal voice. "It's Mandy Miller. . . . I'm fine," she said, suppressing a giggle. "How are you? . . . That's good," she said. "Uh, well, I'm calling because—Hang on a minute."

Ellen covered the mouthpiece with her hand and turned to us. "I don't think I can go through with this. It's not really nice to do this to Mandy."

Kimberly looked at her with a stone-cold face. "Mandy is our declared enemy," she said. "Don't wimp out on us. Act like a real Unicorn."

Ellen took a deep breath. "I'm back," she said into the phone. "I was saying that the reason I'm calling is that I thought you should know something." Lila, Kimberly, and I tried to smother our giggles. For a second Ellen looked like she was about to crack up, too. She turned her back to us. "What did I think you should know?" she asked. "That I, uh, still really like you and I've never gotten over breaking up with you. That's it. Bye." Ellen hung up the phone and we all burst into hysterical laughter.

"Now Rick's going to think Mandy's the biggest geek in the school," Kimberly said.

"That's for sure," Lila agreed. "You sounded like a total moron."

"Do you think I sounded like Mandy?" Ellen asked.

We were silent for a second. The truth was, she'd sounded nothing at all like Mandy. Mandy didn't sound half that geeky. If Mandy *did* call Rick, she'd probably say something funny and really cool.

Not that I think Mandy's so great or anything. It's just that Ellen sounded nothing like her.

"Well, you definitely didn't sound like yourself," Kimberly said finally. "Who wants to go next?"

"I guess I might as well get it over with," Lila said.

"Truth or dare?" Kimberly asked.

"Truth," Lila said.

"OK, who do you think should be president of the Unicorns?" Kimberly asked.

I did a double take. How could she bring up such a loaded subject in such a stupid way? What was she up to?

"Well, to tell you the truth," Lila started, "I'm glad you brought this up."

"Oh, really?" I asked.

"Yeah. I've thought about it a lot and I think I should be the president," Lila said.

"*You?*" I asked her.

Lila put her hands on her hips. "I don't see why you're looking so shocked, Jessica. Why *not* me?"

"Well, it's just that I think I'd make a better Unicorn president, that's all," I replied.

"Oh, boy," Ellen groaned. "I feel like I've already watched this movie and I don't think I'm going to like it better the second time around."

"I don't want another big fight," I said, remembering the horrible competition between me and Lila earlier in the year. "But I really think I'd be the best president. I have all kinds of ideas for the future—"

"And so do I," Lila interrupted. "Don't forget, this slumber party is at my house and, as usual, I've been a really great hostess."

I practically choked on my doughnut. "Wait a minute," I said. "Are you saying that you should be president just because we had our slumber party here?"

"I'm saying that's one of the reasons I should be president," Lila said. "I mean, we spend more time hanging out at my house than we do at anyone else's house."

I rolled my eyes. "Well, it's not like we *have* to hang out here all the time, you know. We can hold meetings and stuff just as often at my house."

"No offense, Jessica, but there's an obvious reason that people prefer being at my house," Lila said.

Have I ever mentioned how much I hate it when she speaks in that annoying superior voice? I felt my whole body start to shake from anger. "Are you saying that something's wrong with my house?"

"This is perfect," Kimberly said, smiling.

"What's perfect?" Ellen asked. "World War Three just broke out."

"I knew this would happen," Kimberly said

smugly. "This is the perfect example of why *I* should be the president of the Unicorns."

"I'm not following you," I said.

"Neither am I," Lila said. "What's your point, Kimberly?"

"There's no way either one of you would accept the other one being president," Kimberly said calmly. "And I don't think you guys really want a replay of what you went through earlier this year."

"You can say that again," Ellen said. "Talk about a major bummer."

"So the solution is simple," Kimberly said. "I should be the president."

"You think you should be the president just so Lila and I don't get into another big competition?" I asked.

"That's one reason," Kimberly said. "But it's not the only one."

"And what's another reason?" Lila asked.

"I represent the way the Unicorns used to be," Kimberly said calmly. "The way we should be now—more fun than the way you guys were earlier in the year."

"But we were all Unicorns last year, too," I pointed out. "It's not like you were the only one."

"Yeah, well, I guess you guys are having some trouble remembering what we were like last year," Kimberly said airily. "You need someone to guide you so you don't mess up and forget what it means to be a real Unicorn."

Oh, please! I said to myself. It sounded like she

thought she had special powers or something. "Kimberly, that's the most ridiculous—"

"There's only one thing to do," Kimberly cut in. "Ellen, I guess you'll have to be the one to settle this."

Ellen's eyes widened as she looked at the three of us. I think I even saw her lip quiver. "I can't make that decision right now. No matter what I say, everyone else will be mad at me."

"So how will we decide?" Lila asked.

I rubbed my forehead. This whole president business was starting to give me a headache. "Let's just drop the subject for now," I suggested. "We can talk about it again later."

"I think I figured out number five," I said.

We were sitting around a table in my backyard on Sunday afternoon, and if you can believe it, we were doing our math homework. In other words, we were running out of activities. I could just imagine how Jessica would tease us if she saw us. Not that there was any chance she *would* see us, of course, since she was at Lila's having the time of her life.

"That's the one I'm having trouble with," Maria said. "Can you give me a hint?"

"I'll just say that the answer is easier than you think," I said.

"Gee, Elizabeth, that really helps," Maria said.

"Are we the biggest losers in Sweet Valley?" Mandy asked.

Evie looked up from her notebook. Since she

didn't have the same homework assignment we did, she was making up her own problems to solve. "What do you mean?" she asked.

"Well, here we are at a slumber party and we're doing our homework," Mandy said, slamming her book closed. "The Unicorns would have a fit if they could see us now."

"That's just what I was thinking," I admitted. I closed my book and poured myself a tall glass of lemonade.

"Let's talk about the future of the Angels," Mandy said. "We've barely done any club business since we got here."

Mary cleared her throat. "OK, let's call an official Angels meeting," she said. "I'll take notes."

"I've got a list here of activities for the future," Mandy said, pulling a sheet of paper out of her notebook. "I've written down a bunch of different kinds of parties that I think we should throw."

I glanced over at Mandy's sheet of paper, which was covered from top to bottom with her ideas. I felt a little bead of perspiration developing on my forehead, and I didn't think it was from the sun.

"Hmm. Maybe someday we'll be presentable enough to go to a party again," Evie said wistfully.

"We definitely will be," Mandy said, rustling her sheet of paper. "I think our spots are actually starting to go away." She cleared her throat. "Now, the first idea I had was to have a sort of old-movie type party. I thought everyone could come dressed as their favorite character from an old movie."

"That sounds fun," Mary said. "But do you think any guys would show up? I mean, I'd bet most of the guys we know have never watched an old movie in their whole lives."

"Good point," Mandy said, making some notes. "We'll make it a party for all kinds of movie characters—modern and old."

Evie smiled. "I think I'll go as Ingrid Bergman's character in *Casablanca*."

"Great," Mandy said. "And speaking of clothes, I think we all should wear our T-shirts to school at least once a week. We can talk on the phone the night before and decide which day we'll wear them."

I felt a little flicker of irritation. She *did* have some good ideas. I just wished she didn't always assume she was in charge. "Mandy, I can see you've been doing a lot of thinking about this stuff," I began.

Mandy smiled proudly. "Yes, I have, as a matter of fact," she said. "I think it's my duty as president to devote some time to this club's future."

I cleared my throat. "As president?"

"Yeah, as president," she replied. "So, anyway, my next idea—"

"Excuse me, Mandy," I broke in, my heart beating hard.

"Question, Elizabeth?" Mandy asked me in a businesslike voice.

"I was just thinking—shouldn't we take a vote?" I asked. "About who's going to be president, I mean."

"Why would we take a vote?" Mandy asked, her eyebrows shooting up. "I *was* elected president this year."

"You were elected president of the Unicorns," I said slowly. "But since the Angels are a new club, I think we should have a new vote. Just in case somebody else wants to be president or something."

"Somebody else?" Mandy repeated, as though she'd never heard those words before. "Who else wants to be president?"

"Not me," Mary said. "I'm going to have my hands full being president of the student council. The last thing I need is to take on another big responsibility."

"Anybody else?" Mandy asked.

"I'm already pretty busy with the paper and my homework," Maria said.

"Since I'm new, I don't really think I should be president," Evie said.

"Well, it looks like I'm the only one who wants the job," Mandy announced.

"Wait a minute," I said. "There's one person who hasn't said if they're interested yet."

Mandy's jaw dropped open. "*You* want to be president?"

"Yes, I do," I stated. "Why do you look so surprised?"

Mandy shrugged. "I just never thought it would be your kind of thing. I mean, you weren't so psyched to join the Unicorns at the beginning."

"But the Unicorns aren't the Angels," I said.

"And I have a lot of good ideas about how to make the club even better than it already is. In fact, I've made a list, too."

Mandy leaned back in her chair. "OK, then. Why don't you tell us some of your ideas?" she said.

I looked around the table and felt everyone's eyes focused on me. I hated being on the spot like that. "Right now?" I asked.

"Sure. Why not?" Mandy asked.

"Well, I don't want to do it now," I said. "It would feel too much like we were having a presidential debate or something. And besides, my list is upstairs."

"Suit yourself," she said matter-of-factly. "We'll talk about this later."

"Yeah . . . later," I repeated.

Ten

"Who has *Fashion Today?*" Kimberly asked, shutting her copy of *Teen Chic*.

"Search me," Ellen said, rolling onto her stomach.

It was Sunday afternoon and we were lying around Lila's bedroom, reading magazines. Luckily Mr. Fowler had gone out that morning to buy a whole new batch. We'd already gone through a huge stack of them the day before.

I never thought I'd say this, but I was getting pretty tired of looking at all those glossy pictures. Still, at least we hadn't been getting into any more fights over who would get to be club president.

"Lila, do you have *Fashion Today?*" Kimberly asked.

"No," Lila answered, turning a page in her magazine.

"Well, do you have any idea where it is?" Kimberly pressed.

Lila looked up from her magazine and sighed. "Kimberly, we don't know where the stupid magazine is. Why don't you read another one?"

"I've read them all already," Kimberly complained. She stretched out on the floor, cupping her chin in her hands. "I guess there weren't that many to begin with."

"Are you complaining that my dad should have bought more magazines?" Lila asked, sitting up.

"I didn't say that," Kimberly snapped.

"I can't believe you're so ungrateful," Lila continued. "My dad and I have been great hosts all weekend."

"Who's saying you haven't?" Ellen asked. "You've been really nice to us."

"My dad rented about a zillion movies for all of us," Lila went on in a quivering voice. "And he's ordered us some of the best gourmet food in all of Sweet Valley."

"Lila, calm down," I said. "I'm sure Kimberly didn't mean to imply that your dad hasn't treated us well. I mean, he's really been wonderful. Kimberly just comes across as a little rude sometimes."

Kimberly stood up and put her hands on her hips. "I can't believe you just said that, Jessica," she yelled. "I never said anything rude or insulting about Lila or her father."

"It certainly sounded that way to me," Lila said, sniffing.

Just then Mrs. Pervis walked in the room. "Jessica, you have a phone call," she said. "It's your sister."

I jumped up eagerly. "Thanks. I'll take it downstairs," I said quickly.

"You can use the phone in my room," Lila suggested.

"That's OK. I don't want to bother you guys," I said.

"You're not going to talk to her, are you?" Kimberly asked.

"Of course I am," I said, walking toward the door.

"But you can't," Kimberly commanded. "She's an Angel. I really think we have to set some kind of rules about interacting with the Angels."

I turned around and stared at Kimberly, exasperated. "You know what?" I said. "I think you should take your rules and stuff them." Then I turned and left the room.

By the time I reached the phone in Lila's basement I was completely out of breath from running down the stairs. "Hello?" I gasped.

"Hi, it's me," Elizabeth said in a weak voice.

"Hi, Elizabeth," I said, trying to sound calm.

"How are you?"

I summoned my chirpiest voice. "Fantastic! What's up?"

"Huh?"

"Why are you calling me?"

"Oh, I, uh, was trying to find my pink oxford shirt and I thought you might know where it is," she said.

"I have no idea," I lied. Actually, it just so happened that I was wearing her pink oxford at that moment. Unfortunately I'd also been wearing it when we'd had hot-fudge sundaes earlier that day, and there was a big chocolate stain right on the front of it.

"Well, the last time I saw it, you were carrying it into your room," she said. "And I don't remember your asking me if you could borrow it."

"Look, I don't know anything about your shirt," I said in a huff. "And you're calling at a bad time."

"Oh? Why's that?"

"We were just in the middle of doing something really fun," I said. "So if you don't have any other questions—"

"What are you doing?" she asked.

Jeez, I thought, *Elizabeth can be so nosy sometimes!* "Oh, you know. Stuff," I said evasively.

"Like what kind of stuff?"

"Right now we're sorting through a bunch of invitations to parties that are coming up," I lied.

"Oh," she practically whispered.

"Anything else you need to know?" I asked impatiently. "I really have to go now."

"Fine," she said curtly. "Bye."

"Bye."

"Guess what, girls?" My mom came into the kitchen on Monday morning as we were eating French toast. "I just talked to the doctor and he said you can all go home now."

I clapped my hands together. "That's great!" I

glanced around and noticed everyone looking at me. "I mean, it's great that we're all better now."

"For a minute I thought you meant it was great we were all leaving," Mandy said, raising an eyebrow.

I forced a laugh. "Of course not," I said. "I'm totally depressed that you're leaving. I'm just glad we're not sick anymore."

"Yeah, it *is* pretty awesome," Mary said. "I mean, that we're not sick anymore. Like Elizabeth said, it's a total bummer that our slumber party's over."

"Yeah, I sort of thought this would be the never-ending sleepover," Maria said, jumping up from the table. "Well, all good things must come to an end, right?"

"So does that mean we can go to school today?" Evie asked excitedly.

"No, you still have to recuperate for a couple more days," my mom said. "But you can do that at your own homes now."

"Will Jessica be coming home, then?" I asked, noticing that my voice sounded strangely eager.

"Yes. I just talked to her," my mom said. "She'll be here soon. Your father just left to go get her."

"Oh," I said, covering my smile with my hand. "That's nice."

"Well, I guess we should gather up our things and call our parents to come get us," Mandy said, getting up from the table. She still had a whole piece of French toast on her plate. "I'm so sad to be leaving."

"Yep, we probably should get on the phone," Maria said. "I'll go first. Might as well get it over with." She practically ran over to the wall and picked up the receiver.

"I guess this is it," Ellen said as we gathered up our sleeping bags and clothes. It was Monday morning and Mr. Fowler had just told us we could all go home.

"Gee, I hate to see you guys go," Lila said cheerfully. She had tried on a floral sundress and was twirling around the room.

"Yeah, it's really too bad," I agreed, throwing my stuff in my bag as quickly as possible.

Kimberly put her hand on her hip and looked at me as if I were a suspect in a detective story or something. "Gee, Jessica, it kind of looks like you can't *wait* to leave."

I turned around to face her. "What makes you say that?"

"You look like you're in a hurry to get out of here," Kimberly replied.

"Well, my dad's going to be here any minute," I said. "So I guess I *am* in a hurry."

"We still haven't resolved the question of who's going to be president," Kimberly said, sitting down on Lila's bed and crossing her legs.

"I seriously doubt we could resolve that right now," Ellen said. "Jessica's right. Our parents will be here any minute."

"Maybe we should set a time to talk about it," Kimberly suggested. "It's not like this issue is going to go away or anything."

"Let's do it later this week, when we're all back in school," Lila said.

"That's a good idea," I said, peering through the window to see if my dad's car was in the drive yet. Unfortunately, it wasn't.

"I'd also like to go by the day-care center later this week," Lila said, fluffing up the pillows on her bed. "I feel terrible that I haven't seen Ellie."

"That sounds great," I said. "I miss Oliver like crazy."

There was a thud from across the room. I looked over and saw that Kimberly had dropped her overnight case on the floor. "I thought you weren't going to go to that stupid place with those bratty kids anymore," she said. She looked incredibly mad.

Lila turned a little pale. "Well, um, I don't think we ever said that—not exactly."

"Well, I think you should say that exactly," Kimberly snapped, her eyes blazing.

"Why?" I demanded. "What's wrong with you?"

Kimberly stood up. "Nothing's wrong with me." She was practically spitting the words. "The problem is with you guys."

"What's wrong with *us*?" Lila asked, wrinkling her forehead.

"You sound like total nerds, the way you're talking about going to that day-care center," she wailed. "I thought that after this weekend you'd go back to the way the Unicorns are *supposed* to be."

I flung my bag over my shoulder. "What exactly are the Unicorns supposed to be like?"

Kimberly picked up one of Lila's pink teddy bears and began choking it. "The way we were last year," she blurted out. "I thought that was the whole reason we broke with the Angels—so we wouldn't do the stupid, immature things you were doing with them earlier this year."

"First of all," I retorted, "we don't think going to the day-care center is immature. Do we?" I turned to Lila and Ellen, who were both staring at the floor. "*Do we?*" I repeated with emphasis. Lila opened her mouth and then closed it.

I stamped my foot. I'd had it—I was sick to death of Kimberly's obnoxious attitude, and I was sick of how Lila and Ellen treated her like some kind of queen. Most of all, I was sick of not saying what I *really* felt. "This is great. Kimberly's calling us immature just because we like hanging out with Oliver and Ellie and the others, and you guys are letting her get away with it. I thought those kids meant more to you than that."

Lila snapped her head up. "They *do* mean more." Her lip began to quiver as she looked at Kimberly. "We're not immature. Going to the day-care center doesn't make us immature."

Ellen straightened up. "No," she said. "It doesn't."

Kimberly's eyes were narrow with anger, but I gave her my fiercest look. "And I think you should remember that *you're* the only reason we're not with the Angels anymore," I said, feeling my temper rise.

"How can you say that?" Kimberly gasped.

"Jessica's right," Lila said, rushing over and

grabbing her teddy bear from Kimberly's clutches. "If it weren't for you, we'd all still be one big Unicorn club."

Kimberly's jaw was practically hanging down to her stomach. "Ellen, do you think the same ridiculous thing?"

Ellen looked at me and then at Lila. "Yeah, I do," she said, almost under her breath.

"How can you say such a thing?" Kimberly demanded. "How is it all my fault?"

"I can't believe you're even asking that question," I shouted. "You're the one who stole Mary's campaign speech."

"But you were all in on that with me," Kimberly shouted back.

"Well, that's different," Lila spat out. "You pretty much pushed us into going along with you."

"And not only that," Ellen added. "As soon as you got back to town, you were trying to make everyone take sides."

"What are you talking about?" Kimberly demanded.

"You were so competitive with Mary," Lila finished for her. "And you had bad things to say about Elizabeth, Maria, and Evie all the time—even though it was obvious they were all our friends. Not to mention the fact that Elizabeth is Jessica's sister."

"Yeah," I said, feeling a new surge of anger. "I don't know how I've been able to stand your horrible company, especially the way you've been picking on my sister."

"It's not just you, Jessica," Lila said furiously, glaring at Kimberly. "We've all let her stick her nose in where she's not wanted."

"What are you talking about?" Kimberly demanded. "You're all acting totally crazy."

"Let me interpret," I told her through clenched teeth. "I think what we're all saying is that we were happy with the way things were before you got here. All you did by coming back to Sweet Valley was mess everything up."

"Are you saying that you guys still want to be with that group of geeks?" Kimberly asked, looking as though she might topple over. "Well? Do you?" she pressed when no one said anything.

"I don't know," Lila said, shifting from one foot to the other. "Maybe."

"So all this time you guys have been resenting me for breaking up the group?" Kimberly asked, her lip trembling.

"Yes," Lila said softly.

Ellen nodded.

"*What?*" Kimberly asked. "What did you just say?"

"She said yes!" I exclaimed loudly. "They both said yes. Yes, yes, yes, we wish you had never come back!"

For a moment Kimberly looked as if she wanted to clobber me. Then she did something I thought she'd never do. Her face crumbled and her whole body shook with huge, wailing sobs. She collapsed in a heap on Lila's bed. "*That's* why I don't want you to go to the day-care center," she cried.

"Why?" Ellen asked, looking flustered. "What's why?"

"Because . . . because it's something you did while I was gone," Kimberly said in a whimper.

"But there's no reason you couldn't go there, too," Lila protested. "You're acting like a baby."

"I just want things to be the way they used to be," Kimberly said, looking up through her tears. "I want us to be like the old Unicorns."

Lila and I exchanged glances.

"When I came back to Sweet Valley, I felt like everything had changed," Kimberly went on, her voice shaking. "It seemed like everything had gone on fine without me. There were three new Unicorns and your whole philosophy was different."

"You mean because we were working at the day-care center?" I asked softly.

"Yeah," Kimberly said. "In the old days, you never would have cared about some poor kids. I just sort of felt left out." Fresh tears coursed down her face. "And I can see I was right. You've all said it—you think the club would be better off without me."

"Jessica! Your father's here!" Mr. Fowler yelled from downstairs.

I let out all my breath. I knew that leaving just then, with Kimberly so upset, was kind of a crummy thing to do, but I was pretty glad to be let off the hook. "Wow, sorry," I said, grabbing my stuff. "I guess we'll just have to continue this when we're back at school. See you guys later! Thanks for the, um, slumber party, Lila!"

I ran out of the room and thundered down the stairs. I couldn't wait to see my dad.

Eleven

"Hi," Jessica said tentatively, standing in the door-way of my room. It was Monday morning and I was sitting on my bed, reading a mystery.

"Oh, hi," I said cautiously. "What did you do to your hair?"

"I thought I'd try something new," she said, pull-ing her curly hair back with her hands.

"Yeah, well, it's different, that's for sure," I said, trying to pry my eyes from the enormous mass of curls. Her hair *was* different—different from mine.

"Um, I was wondering if you'd seen my purple robe," she said.

"No, I haven't," I said briskly, looking back at my book.

"Oh, OK," she said. "I'll let you get back to your reading, then."

"OK. Bye," I mumbled, staring at the words on the page.

"Bye."

I could feel her looking at me for a moment before she turned to leave.

"Wait," I said quickly.

She turned around. "What is it?"

"How was your party?" I asked.

"Oh, it was really great," she said, smiling widely. "Too bad it's over. How was yours?"

"It was a blast," I said, managing a smile.

Jessica twisted a strand of her curly hair around her finger. "Yeah, I was really sorry to have to leave," she said again.

I sighed dramatically. "I know what you mean. I wish my friends didn't have to go."

"It's cool we get to stay home from school today," Jessica said, taking one step closer to my bed.

"Yeah, I guess so," I said.

"So, what do you think you'll do today?" Jessica asked.

"I'll probably read. What about you?"

"Hmm, I don't know. . . . I wouldn't mind playing a game or something," she said, looking at her hands.

"Like maybe Monopoly or something?" I suggested in a small voice.

"Something like that," Jessica said, grabbing the game from my desk and carrying it to my bed.

"But you have to promise that you won't cheat," I

said, knowing full well that that was exactly what she was going to do.

"I promise!"

"OK, she's the one who had that brain tumor," I explained to Elizabeth, pointing at the television screen. It was Monday afternoon and Elizabeth and I were watching *Days of Turmoil*, my favorite soap opera, in the family room.

"Who has a brain tumor?" Mom asked, appearing in the doorway.

Elizabeth and I giggled. "The woman on the TV, Mom," Elizabeth said. "Not a real person."

"How come you're not at work?" I asked.

"I came home for lunch to fix you your favorite sick-day meal," Mom said. "Hang on, I'll be right back."

Elizabeth got up to unfold two TV trays and set them up in front of the couch.

"This is my favorite kind of day," I said.

"Me, too," Elizabeth said. "Even if you did beat me at Monopoly."

Mom walked back in carrying a tray of grilled cheese sandwiches, tomato soup, and glasses of milk. She's been making that lunch for us when we're sick ever since we were little girls.

"Here you go," Mom said.

"Thanks, Mom. You're the best," Elizabeth said.

"I think this has to be the most comforting meal in the world," I said, putting my face over my bowl to breathe in the fragrant steam from the soup.

"How are you girls feeling?" Mom asked.

"Much better," Elizabeth said.

"How about you, Jessica?" Mom asked.

I winked at Elizabeth. "Actually, I'm not feeling all that great," I said, making my best sick-kid face. "I'd say I'll definitely have to stay home from school this whole week. Maybe even next week, too."

Mom folded her arms and smiled. "Well, maybe you'll feel better after you eat. I have to get back to the office. I'll call you later to check in."

"OK. Thanks again, Mom," Elizabeth said.

"Oh, and don't watch TV all afternoon," Mom said as she walked out the door.

"We won't," I called after her. I glanced at Elizabeth. "What she doesn't know won't hurt her."

Elizabeth laughed and blew on a spoonful of soup. "You know, I'm not feeling so great myself."

"You're not?" I asked.

"Nope," she said, smiling. "In fact, I think I might have to stay at home for the next week or two also. Oh, well." She shrugged. "Might as well make the best of it."

I grinned. "Here's to being sick," I said, raising my milk glass.

"To being sick," she echoed, clinking her glass against mine.

"I bet you girls are looking forward to getting back to school," Dad said at breakfast on Wednesday morning.

"I guess," Jessica said, pushing her waffles around on her plate.

"Sure," I said, tracing a pattern in my syrup with my fork.

Part of me *was* sort of looking forward to going to school, but the other part was dreading it. Going back to school meant not hanging out with Jessica anymore. I'd be with the Angels and she'd be with the Unicorns. The two of us had had so much fun together over the past couple of days that it made me sad to have that time end.

"At least your spots are all gone," Steven said, helping himself to more waffles. "Although it would have been fun to take a Magic Marker and connect the dots." He snapped his fingers. "Too bad I didn't think of that till now."

"Har-dee-har-har," Jessica said, rolling her eyes.

"Jessica, I think we should get a Magic Marker and connect the two new pimples Steven woke up with this morning," I said, giggling into my napkin.

Steven picked up a fork and tried to see his reflection. "What new pimples?" he asked in a panic.

Jessica looked at me and we cracked up. Steven is super sensitive about his acne, and Jessica and I love to tease him about it.

"Are you sure we're not still contagious?" I asked.

"The doctor said you should be one hundred percent better by now," Mom said.

"I'm not sure he's one hundred percent right, Mom," Jessica said. She yawned dramatically. "I'm *desperately* tired."

"Well, then, maybe you should come right home after school and take a nap," Dad said.

Jessica furrowed her brow. "After school? Oh, I'm sure I'll feel much better by then," she said quickly.

Dad looked at his watch and stood up from the table. "It's time to go," he said. "I can drop you off at school on my way to the office."

Jessica and I looked at each other and smiled weakly. We didn't have to say anything—each of us just knew that the other was feeling the same way.

"I know it's only been a couple of days, but I feel like we've been away from here for weeks," Lila said at the Unicorner on Wednesday.

"I know what you mean," Ellen agreed. "I guess it just seemed longer than it was. I was so bored at my house, I thought I was going out of my mind."

Just then I spotted Kimberly coming toward the Unicorner with her tray. "Here comes Kimberly," I whispered. "Did I miss anything after I left on Monday?"

"No. Our parents came a few seconds later," Ellen said.

Kimberly stopped a few feet from our table. "What are you guys whispering about?" she asked.

I cleared my throat and tossed my *straight* hair over my shoulder. (I'd shampooed it ten times the day before, so it was back to normal.) "Nothing," I said. "Aren't you going to sit down with us?"

"Are you sure you want me to?" she asked, looking down at the mashed potatoes on her plate.

"Of course we do," Lila said, pulling out a chair for her. "Don't be silly."

Kimberly hesitated and then slowly lowered herself into a chair. "That's a really pretty shirt you're wearing, Jessica," she said.

I looked down at the purple blouse I had on. "Thanks," I said. "My mom gave it to me for my last birthday."

"Ellen, you gave a great answer in English class this morning," Kimberly said. "I was really impressed."

"You were?" Ellen asked, looking surprised. "I didn't think anyone was paying attention."

"Are you kidding? You sounded amazing," Kimberly told her.

"Well, thanks," Ellen said, smiling. "I did all the reading for class while I was home sick, since there was nothing else to do."

"Lila, I want to send a thank-you note to you and your dad," Kimberly went on. "Both of you were really gracious and everything this weekend. I really appreciate it."

Lila looked up from her sloppy joe sandwich. "You don't have to send a note," she said. "But it's a nice thought."

I stared at my meat loaf and mashed potatoes. Lila was right—Kimberly *was* being extra nice. And I, for one, couldn't figure out what to say to her—I just wasn't used to her acting thoughtful.

"Hi, guys."

I looked up from my food to see Evie standing by our table, smiling timidly.

"Hi!" I said in an unexpectedly friendly-sounding voice. Lila immediately sent me a look that said, *Don't be so nice to the enemy.*

Evie wrung her hands together nervously. "Uh, Lila, I just wanted to tell you that . . . uh . . . Ellie really misses you and she asked me to tell you that," she stammered.

Lila's face broke into a wide grin. "Really?" she asked happily. "When did she say that?"

Evie seemed to relax a little bit. "I stopped by the day-care center yesterday to drop off some dress-up clothes from my grandmother's store," she explained. "Ellie was really excited, and right away she put on a red velvet dress. She kept saying, 'I look like Lila now.'"

Lila laughed. "That's too adorable!"

"Well, anyway, I just thought I should tell you that, since I promised Ellie," Evie said, turning to walk away.

"Wait, Evie," I called out. "Did Oliver say anything about me?"

"Actually, he asked if you'd gone away or something," Evie said.

"What did you tell him?" I asked.

"I said you were probably just busy," Evie said.

"Oh, OK," I said softly. "Thanks."

"Well, see ya," Evie said, heading off.

"I have an idea," Lila announced, her eyes lighting up. "Let's go to the day-care center this afternoon."

Kimberly frowned. "I thought maybe we could all go shopping or something," she said.

All of a sudden I missed the kids so much that my chest ached. "You can go shopping, but I'm going to the center with Lila," I said firmly. "I just want to see how Oliver's doing. I mean, if he's asking about me and everything, I should go say hi."

"Why don't you come with us?" Ellen suggested to Kimberly.

"That's a great idea," Lila said. "Maybe you'll really like it there and you'll want to start going there regularly with us."

Kimberly made a doubtful face. "What exactly do you do there?"

"We just play games and read stories and stuff," I said. "It's really fun."

"Do they get, like, paint and juice on your clothes?" Kimberly asked, wrinkling her nose.

I had to laugh. "Sometimes they get a little messy," I said. "But it's not that bad."

"Won't the Angels be there?" Kimberly asked.

"Yeah, probably, but that's OK," Lila said. "I mean, we can just hang out with the kids. We don't have to do stuff with the Angels."

"I don't know." Kimberly hesitated. "Do you think the kids will like me? I mean, I'm not all that good with kids."

Wow! She really was insecure. It's so funny how somebody can come across as completely self-assured, even conceited, and then it turns out that they have no self-confidence.

"Kimberly, they're just kids," I said. "And most of them come from pretty poor families. They're just so happy to have people like us there to play with them. They'll be psyched to have a new person there."

"Come on," Ellen urged. "Just say you'll come with us."

Kimberly was shredding her paper napkin. "What about the Angels? They all hate me because of the election."

"It doesn't matter what they think," Lila said. "You're going with us, and we don't hate you."

Kimberly sighed. "OK, I'll come," she said. "But I won't promise that I'll like it."

"I can't believe it," Mary said, putting her tray down at the Angeliner. "Jessica just smiled at me."

"Are you sure she didn't have something in her eye?" Mandy asked.

"No, I'm positive," Mary said. "It was definitely a smile. And it was directed at me."

"I don't think it's *that* hard to believe," I said a little defensively.

"Get real, Elizabeth," Mary said, rolling her eyes. "When was the last time that Jessica or any Unicorn smiled at an Angel?"

"You know, it's funny, but now that you mention it, Ellen let me go in front of her in the lunch line," Maria said, spearing a few peas with her fork.

Mandy rested her chin against her fist, looking thoughtful. "Lila actually said something that sounded like hi in social studies this morning."

"Do you think they're up to something?" Maria asked suspiciously.

"You mean like a prank?" Mandy asked. "I don't know. Anything's possible with the Unicorns."

"What do you think, Elizabeth?" Evie asked. "Did Jessica say anything about a Unicorn scheme when you were home with her these last two days?"

"It was strange, actually," I said. "We didn't talk about the war between the Unicorns and the Angels at all. In fact, the two of us got along really well. Just like old times."

"Maybe they're beginning to realize how wrong they were about all that election stuff," Mary said.

"Let's not get carried away here," Maria said. "So they said hi to us. I don't think we should expect to see a white flag just yet. One thing I've learned this year is never to trust a Unicorn."

"Lila!" Ellie squealed as she ran across the room.

The Angels and I were at the day-care center on Wednesday afternoon, playing a rousing game of duck duck goose, and the Unicorns had just walked through the door.

"Am I seeing things?" Maria whispered to me.

"There's nothing wrong with your vision," I said. "All the Unicorns just arrived—even Kimberly."

"Hi, Oliver!" Jessica exclaimed as he ran into her arms. "I brought this book for you. It's about a little train engine. I know you like trains."

"Thanks," Oliver said excitedly. "Where have you been? I missed you."

"I missed you, too," Jessica said. "Hi, Elizabeth."

I couldn't help smiling. "Hi. We were just playing duck duck goose. Do you guys want to join us?"

"You're kidding, right?" Kimberly asked, smirking. Since coming in she'd been standing in the doorway with her arms crossed defiantly in front of her.

"No joke," Maria said flatly. "We're playing duck duck goose. Take it or leave it."

"Come on, Lila," Ellie said, pulling on Lila's dress. "Play with us."

"You're not actually considering playing, are you?" Kimberly asked.

"Please, Jessica," Oliver pleaded.

"Sure, why not?" Jessica said, laughing, as Oliver led her across the floor.

Ellie stood between Lila and Ellen, tugging on their hands.

"OK, OK," Lila said with a chuckle as she and Ellen sat down.

Kimberly looked like she was about to faint. "You guys aren't embarrassed to play that silly game?" she asked. "I mean, it's so babyish."

"It's fun," Arthur said, walking over to Kimberly. He took her hand and led her toward the circle. "Try it."

"I don't want to play," Kimberly said, sounding like a four-year-old.

Maria looked at me and we both giggled.

"Well, you'll be the only one not playing," Mandy said.

"Please play with us," Ellie said in the sweetest voice you can imagine.

Kimberly looked down at little Ellie and her lips

twitched in a smile. "OK, but I'm not sitting on the floor," she said. She pulled a tiny chair from one of the arts-and-crafts tables and placed it in the circle. She sat down on it and crossed her legs.

"I'll go first," Ellie announced. She started walking around the circle slowly, placing her hand on each head, saying, "Duck, duck, duck . . ."

When she got around to Kimberly, she put her hand on Kimberly's head and yelled out, "*Goose!*"

Kimberly's face turned bright red.

Jessica slapped her hand over her mouth, and Lila and Ellen began shaking with giggles.

"You don't really expect me to go through with this, do you?" Kimberly asked, scrunching up her face.

"Come on!" Ellie shrieked. "You have to chase me!"

"But I haven't done this since I was six years old!" Kimberly protested.

Ellie was running around the circle by herself, smiling even though nobody was chasing her.

"It you don't catch her, you'll have to sit in the middle," I said through my own laughter.

"Oh, OK," Kimberly said grudgingly. She stood slowly and walked around the circle.

Ellie plopped down in Kimberly's seat and squealed with delight. "You're it now!" she yelled to Kimberly.

Kimberly turned pale, and for a moment I thought she'd run right out of the center. But instead she did something totally unexpected. She heaved a huge sigh and began walking around the circle, putting her hand on everyone's head. "Duck, duck, duck . . ."

"Wasn't that fun?" I asked Kimberly later that afternoon as we walked home. "Aren't the kids great?"

Kimberly pushed her hair behind her ear. "I guess."

"You guess?" Lila asked with a giggle. "You looked like you were having fun."

"Come on, Kimberly, admit it," I said. "You loved it when Yuki was braiding your hair."

"Well, I suppose it wasn't totally disgusting," Kimberly admitted. Her hair was still braided; it looked cute on her. "If you're into that sort of thing. Of course, I'm still not sure this is a real Unicorn activity."

"What exactly is a real Unicorn activity?" I asked.

"You'll see," Kimberly replied mysteriously.

What does Kimberly have up her sleeve for the Unicorns? Find out in The Unicorn Club #8, Kimberly Rides Again.

SIGN UP FOR THE SWEET VALLEY HIGH® FAN CLUB!

Hey, girls! Get all the gossip on Sweet Valley High's® most popular teenagers when you join our fantastic Fan Club! As a member, you'll get all of this really cool stuff:

- Membership Card with your own personal Fan Club ID number
- A Sweet Valley High® Secret Treasure Box
- Sweet Valley High® Stationery
- Official Fan Club Pencil (for secret note writing!)
- Three Bookmarks
- A "Members Only" Door Hanger
- Two Skeins of J. & P. Coats® Embroidery Floss with flower barrette instruction leaflet
- Two editions of *The Oracle* newsletter
- Plus exclusive Sweet Valley High® product offers, special savings, contests, and much more!

Be the first to find out what Jessica & Elizabeth Wakefield are up to by joining the Sweet Valley High® Fan Club for the one-year membership fee of only $6.25 each for U.S. residents, $8.25 for Canadian residents (U.S. currency). Includes shipping & handling.

Send a check or money order (do not send cash) made payable to "Sweet Valley High® Fan Club" along with this form to:

SWEET VALLEY HIGH® FAN CLUB, BOX 3919-B, SCHAUMBURG, IL 60168-3919

NAME_____
(Please print clearly)

ADDRESS_____

CITY_____ STATE_____ ZIP_____
(Required)

AGE_____ BIRTHDAY_____ /_____ /_____